Bread and Tea

ARABIC LITERATURE & LANGUAGE SERIES

The Arabic Literature and Language series serves to make available Arabic literature and educational material to the general public as well as academic faculty, students, and institutions in collaboration with local Arab writers from the region. The series will focus on publishing Arabic literature translated into English from less commonly translated regions of the Arab world and from genres representing vibrant social issues in Arabic literature. The series will make available poetry books in dual languages (Arabic/English), novels, short stories, and anthologies. It will also publish textbooks for teaching Arabic language, literature, and culture, and scholarly works about the region.

SERIES EDITOR

Nesreen Akhtarkhavari, *DePaul University*

Bread and Tea

The Story of a Man from Karak

Ahmad Tarawneh

Translated by

Nesreen Akhtarkhavari

Michigan State University Press | *East Lansing*

Michigan State University Press
East Lansing, Michigan 48823-5245

Supported by Ministry of Culture of
The Hashemite Kingdom of Jordan

2   0   1   7

The publication of this book was partially funded
by a grant from the Jordanian Ministry of Culture.

LIBRARY OF CONGRESS CATALOGING-IN-PUBLICATION DATA
Names: Tarawneh, Ahmad, author. | Akhtarkhavari, Nesreen, translator.
Title: Bread & tea / Ahmad Tarawneh ; translated by Nesreen Akhtarkhavari.
Other titles: Khubzun wa shay. English | Bread and tea
Description: East Lansing : Michigan State University Press, [2021] |
Series: Arabic literature and language series
Identifiers: LCCN 2021019636 | ISBN 9781611862775 (paperback) |
ISBN 9781609175573 (pdf) | ISBN 9781628953251 (epub) | ISBN 9781628963250 (Kindle)
Classification: LCC PJ7964.A73 K4913 2021 | DDC 892.7—dc23
LC record available at https://lccn.loc.gov/2021019636

Cover design by Shaun Allshouse, www.shaunallshouse.com
Cover art: Kerak, by Berthold Werner, Wikicommons

Visit Michigan State University Press at www.msupress.org

To Basem, my son
The source of joy in my life . . .

Contents

Introduction

About the Author and the Novel

Ahmad Tarawneh is an award-winning Jordanian novelist, screenwriter, and literary critic. *Bread and Tea* (2016) is his second novel. His first novel was *Wadi al-Safsafa*, for which he received Jordan's Literary Award in 2009.

Tarawneh has authored many other literary works, including short stories, plays, essays, biographies, documentaries, and more. His screenplays and scripts have been produced for theater, radio, and television. His work has been published in prominent national and regional publications, including a 2020 short story, *CORONA's Diary*, that won the Jordanian Ministry of Culture Award.

Currently, he is the managing editor of the Literary and Cultural Division of *Al-Ra'i Newspaper*, one of Jordan's oldest and most prominent publications. Previously, he served as the chief editor of *Al-Karak Cultural Journal* published by the Jordanian Cultural Cities Association, and *Aqlam Jadedah* published by the University of Jordan. He has also served as the editor-in-chief of Philadelphia News, a cable broadcast station in Jordan.

Tarawneh is active in the Jordanian and Arab literary scene. He has served in many elected positions on the boards of literary organizations, including as vice president of the Jordanian Writers Society, member of the Arab Writers League, a founding member of The Literary Critics Group, and the Karak Literary Group.

Ahmad Tarawneh is from Karak in the southern region of Jordan with its distinct geography, history, tribes, cultures, and traditions. The identity of the place shapes his perceptions and is strongly reflected in his literary work, including this novel. He sees the novel as a mix of his own understanding of reality and the reality of others. It is a "lantern I carry in a dark night, to spy on my own soul and the souls of the protagonists that run after me, asking me to free them with my pen."* He develops his characters, adding thoughts and ideas, filling the gaps, borrowing from other events that he knows, or creates with his vivid imagination. It is a conscious effort to construct a complete work, careful that the work is comprehensive and clearly influenced by the way the author himself sees things and reads his own reality. He confirms this stating, "I present through it my stand and position toward what life offers us." Yet, it is an independent world that is guided by the modes, virtues, and sins of its own characters, a "new life," which he explains, "I sometimes write to escape my own life and turn to openings in the lives of others. I read through it the universe, with all its details," details that strongly carry the scent of the place, and its movements and colors.

The novel consists of thirty-three chapters. Each chapter has a title that reflects its content. I believe that this is helpful in keeping track of the novel's complex plot and different characters and spaces. The main characters include Abu Ahmad and his brother, Abu Khalil, who contributed in the past to protecting the nation during their prime. They are the main characters during the first half of the novel. They are forced

---

* Unpublished interview with Ahmad Tarawneh, conducted by Nesreen Akhtarkhavari on December 5, 2020. All the author's comments in this introduction are based on this interview, unless otherwise specified.

in their old age to dig for artifacts to support their families, facing poverty in a life that is reduced to only affording "bread and tea," the title of the novel, a common reference to poverty in Jordanian culture. The sudden death of Abu Ahmad, after finding a valuable relic, and the greed of his brother, Abu Khalil, who is manipulated by Yusuf, the history teacher, starts a series of events and disappointments. In the absence of the voice of Jamal, the antiquities expert, who seems to care about the nation and its treasures, Abu Khalil falls under the influence of Yusuf and becomes just as ruthless and greedy. This leads Abu Ahmad's sons, Ahmad and Khalid, to choose different paths in their quest for self-control, influence, and strength to take revenge on their uncle and his handler, the history teacher.

The other main characters in the novel stay nameless. They include the sheikhs that recruit and facilitate young Ahmad's involvement with the jihadists, and the Darak, the security forces, that train and prepare young Khalid to be an instrument in the hands of the regime. Tarawneh's female protagonists like Um Ahmad, Abu Ahmad's wife, and Sawsan, the wife of the history teacher, play key roles in developing the central themes of the novel and shedding light on the complex social and cultural gender-based relationships governed by religion, tradition, and social norms.

Other female characters include Khalid's younger sister, and the girls in the minibus at the battlefield in Syria. They are hardly noticeable and play minor roles in the novel. A few other minor characters are introduced during the story like the two men on the bus, the young boy that helps Ahmad read the address where he is directed to carry out his mission, the peculiar man that warns Ahmad that the riot is about to start, and the man waiting for the bus and telling Ahmad about the good times when everyone cared for the country. All the minor characters remain nameless. They serve the story, further the plot, help develop the main characters, but do not distract from the novel's central theme and issues.

Tarawneh shared that the main protagonists in his novel, *Bread and Tea*, are real. He retained their full names and changed them only in the final draft of the manuscript to inspire him to remain focused and keep the story real. He replaced the real names with generic professions or just first names; sometimes he intentionally used both—for example, Yusuf, the history teacher—to remind the reader of the impact professional people have on the development of events and the shaping of a society. Being conscious and true to the Jordanian identity, and in particular, the south, is a common feature of the work of Jordanian novelists, as we see in the work of the father of postmodernist Arabic literature, Tayseer al-Sboul.[†] They carry Jordan and its south in their heart, mind, and on the tip of their pens.

The author sees this novel, *Bread and Tea*, as an intentional and significant study of the social, political, and historical realities of not only Jordan but also the Arab region as a whole. He chooses the south with all its particularness and complexity as the backdrop and stage for the events in the novel and the place from which to depart. The characters in his novel are the products of that environment, linking its past to its present, and charting its future.

The novel is realistic but utilizes mythology and a gothic context in some scenes to intentionally illustrate a point and frame the events. The author chooses to start the novel in a cemetery at a historical site linking the past to the present and presenting the problem of poverty and the social and political predicaments the characters face within the uniqueness of the south itself. He shared with me that he lived for a week with the characters that he wrote about and went with them to the cemetery at night while they were searching for treasures, ate their food, and watched them carry on with their lives. He saw the bones scattered out of the graves, felt the dampness of the soil, inhaled the scent of decaying bodies, and witnessed the excitement of the find. Many of

---

[†] In reference to the renown Jordanian poet and novelist, Tayser al-Sboul and his Arabic postmodernist novel, *You as of Today My Homeland*, translated by Nesreen Akhtarkhavari (East Lansing: Michigan State University Press, 2016).

the events that take place in this novel are the product of that experience and the conversations Tarawneh had with the protagonists themselves, not only the ones that he developed while they lived in his mind but also the one he based the story on and lived with while researching the subject of his novel. Tarawneh remains true to the south and its people even when he introduces dark fantasy scenes, as in the trial of the corpses and skeletons that Ahmad dreams while alone in the cemetery at night guarding the grave his father and uncle had started digging during the day. The scene with its ominous tones, gloomy disposition, and standard features of fantasy was inspired by a conversation Tarawneh had with the actual gravediggers while watching the scattered bones around the cemetery, jokingly suggesting that the skeletons may hold a trial against those who desecrate their graves. The relationship between the place, the objects, and the protagonists, and its display in an authentic cultural context is present throughout the novel, such as the first encounter of the younger brother, Khalid, with the picture of the King and his reaction to the image. The scene symbolizes the complex relationship the Jordanian people, especially in the south, have with the royal family. Traces of this relationship are present throughout the novel, especially when addressing identity.

Another important theme in the novel is the economic exploitation of the poor by various socioeconomic groups at multiple levels of society. Writing about the novel, Hekmat al-Nawaiseh suggests that it is "a narrative constructed from the intricate details of the life experienced by the poor and the big players who see these poor only as subjects to be exploited in all contexts—wealth, religion, or politics."‡ This is a central theme that keeps the pieces of the novel together.

In his article about the book, Ibrahim Khalil calls it, the novel that "condemns terrorism,"§ which Tarawneh skillfully conveyed through dialogue. Khalil praises Tarawneh's dialogue skills and points out to its

---

‡   Hekmat al-Nawaiseh, "Khubz was Shay: Fuqara' wa Athar wa La'iboun Kibar," Alarabi Aljadid, December 10, 2020, alaraby.co.uk.

§   Ibrahim Khalil, "Kubzun wa Shay li-Ahmad Tarawneh: Rewayat al-Tandeed bil-Irhab," November 6, 2016, http://alrai.com/article/792498.html.

dominance in the novel. He goes as far as suggesting that "if you take the dialogue out of Tarawneh's novel [*Bread and Tea*], you will be left with fragments." This is true to a certain degree and could be attributed to Tarawneh's background as a play and television screenwriter, which provides him the ability to see details, and the skill to describe them. Khalil further suggests that the excess use of dialogue by Tarawneh does not impact the well-developed structure of the novel, which maintains smooth transitions between its parts in language and form.

Tarawneh's mastery of the Arabic language is augmented by his knowledge of the culture, intimate familiarity with the place, and his understanding of the issues addressed in the novel. This gives him the abilities and skills needed to mold vivid images and construct descriptions with great details and unique linguistic expressions. Khalil suggests that Tarawneh overloads his work with images and metaphors, which, at times are not necessary to further the plot. But, as Khalil asserts, in the end, this does not interfere with the solid structure of the novel, its well-developed concepts, and skillfully constructed form. Every word in the novel is carefully chosen with hints placed strategically and visually to provide clues and to guide the reader on his journey through the novel. An example is the description of the sheikh, with his red beard, short thoub, and white headcover without an iqal. The red beard suggests that he uses henna dye, which, combined with his short thoub and the absence of an iqal, reveals strong adherence to Muslim conservative practices and indicates the ideology and political affiliation of the character. In another example, the man on the bus who defends the Jordanian Darak (military security forces) wears a red keffiyeh, a symbol of Jordanian identity. These references are scattered throughout the novel, contributing to contextualizing its characters without having to rely on extensive narration.

Tarawneh utilizes place in all its dimensions and scopes through descriptions and metaphors. He further links it to the people and their thoughts and feelings. He turns it into a tool of inspiration to understand self and others, and to form ideas and opinions. For example, the main protagonist in the novel, Ahmad, lays in his mother's lap, watching and analyzing the movement of the stars in the sky, asking her about his life, his circumstances, God, and the universe. Her answer is a call to action. The novel is also the panorama of the place itself, the village with its cemetery, mosques, houses, alleys, and archaeological sites that reveal a history rooted in ancient times, a city familiar and foreign at the same time, its alleys, squares, and endless roads, crossing the heart of the desert to everywhere and nowhere.

Tarawneh's novel has an intelligent message that is meant to inform and impact. It is clearly expressed with the author nudging the characters, and at times, guiding their steps and conversations. Perhaps this is best illustrated in the scene where Ahmad, the young sexually frustrated *mujahid* (fighter) in the middle of a battle in Syria, sees a minibus of women who are there practicing *jihad al-nikah*, providing sexual comfort to the fighters. He gets excited, but then decides that it is not for him. This was brought about by seeing a lock of hair of one of the girls in the group that reminds him of his little sister! The subject is dropped, and Tarawneh chooses not to deal with it, leaving traces of an inhibition, a moral compass, and cultural taboo rooted in the tribal customs that both the author and the protagonist subscribe to.

Bread and Tea is an important novel to make available to English-language readers. In addition to its literary value, it provides the readers with perceptions, philosophies, and the patten of thinking and living of multiple generations of Arabs, especially youth. Ibrahim Khalil lists the novel among important Arabic works that address critical subjects including terrorism. He praises Tarawneh for treating the subject in a unique and effective way through creating an internal dialogue that leads the protagonists to construct a meaningful argument for rejecting the act of terrorism as an end, demonstrating that random and absurd killing does not represent religion or the homeland and that subscribing to it is not a solution to everyday problems. This is an important message critical to understanding radicalization and offering a logic to combat it from within.

The novel does not shy away from dealing with social, religious, and political taboos. It addresses some of the major contradictions, hypocrisies, and the bankruptcy of some of the so-called intellectuals in the Arab world. It describes the forces that influence the minds of young people, both political and religious, and provides an intelligent discourse about the relationship between identity and ideology. The novel thoughtfully leads the reader to realize the need to create role models, to solve social issues, like poverty, corruption, and nepotism, and to make available effective education that provides the youth with the skills needed to succeed in life. He demonstrates that the absence of social justice and the diminishing pastoral role of social, religious, and political institutions force young people to take a path and make decisions that are detrimental not only to them but also to the nation itself. Again, this is not a random message that the novel offers, but an intentional act by the author. Tarawneh clearly expresses that he sees the novel as a tool to influence and bring about change, "a guillotine that is set to execute a reality that contributed to the destruction of this world." The way Tarawneh chooses to execute the "reality" of terrorism is by providing a narrative of its fallacy demonstrated from within.

About the Translation

I read Ahmad Tarawneh's novel *Bread and Tea* in 2017. It was recommended for translation by Jordanian writer colleagues and the Ministry of Culture as a novel that could complement the Jordanian literary works already available in English.

My main concern about translating the novel was its highly descriptive language and heavy use of metaphors and cultural expressions that have little or no equivalent in English.

Stepping out of my role as a translator and reading the novel again convinced me of the importance of making it available in English. The novel's content, internal dialogues, treatment of identity, and the internal discourses about terrorism, in my view, are great contributions, not only to English literature, but also to scholars and practitioners who seek to better understand Arabs and the Arab mind.

I read the novel a few more times until I was in tune with the author's voice. This is essential for me as a translator. It allows me to render the source text from the point of view of the author, trying as much as the English language permits to use his feelings, tone, images, metaphors, language structures, to be able to add and omit when needed, what the author himself would add, not what I, the translator, would like to see. It was not until I developed this level of intimacy with the novel, that I could truly produce a meaningful version in English. Only then, does faithful translation become possible and not just a mechanical act.

Language fascinates me, and I enjoy literary translation from Arabic to English. I constantly think about the English reader, including my students, about what they might learn, and the joy, surprise, disgust, horror, and amazement that they might experience when reading the work. Although this is my eighth published translation of literary work—mainly Jordanian poetry and novels—translating *Bread and Tea* had its own unique challenges. I am not a fan of gothic and horror genres, so I had to learn new content vocabulary to accurately translate the cemetery scenes. I also had to figure out how to treat, in a consistent manner, language repetition, which is a sign of eloquence and is highly tolerated in Arabic but is seen as distracting in English.

To ensure accuracy and allow me to go back and check my translation against the source text, I kept the source text and the target text side by side. After finishing the translation, I edited the text and went back and read it one more time looking for words, idioms, references, and expressions with historical and cultural implications that needed to be further explained to facilitate access to the text and its cultural and contextual references. I utilized the feedback of a number of native speakers of English, including my husband who is familiar with Arab culture, but does not speak Arabic, to identify additional words, expressions, and concepts that would contribute, if further explained, to better understand the text. I went through the manuscript again and included numerous footnotes to ensure readers' access to the text and all its nuances.

In writing the introduction, I came across no reference to the novel in English, but quite a number of reviews and articles in Arabic. To further enrich the introduction, I conducted a virtual interview with the author, in addition to numerous calls and text messages that validated my understanding of his position as a writer and his relationship with the text. This helped me better understand the novel and introduce it to you, the English reader.

I do believe that *Bread and Tea* by Ahmad Tarawneh is a beautiful, relevant, and content-rich novel, full of human encounters that we share as people. It enriches the diversity of the body of literature available in English and contributes to making more Jordanian literature, which is still less commonly translated to English, accessible to English-language readers.

Threshold I

In the midst of darkness, a small opening appeared in the ceiling—a dim light came through it, like a glance, unable to find its way. The sound around him shattered in the hallow of the darkness. Its viscid letters scattered when a breeze of air entered the cylinder-shaped room. He moved slightly away from the opening—his memories were lost in the chains.

Threshold II

At this threshold, here, shake the dust off your clothes if you can, just as Ahmad shook the dust of falsehood off his shirt.

You will not be able to, and you will continue to see yourself above the truth. I know that, because Ahmad is the one who wrote my novel and will be writing yours when the land turns barren, and the lights are extinguished. Darkness will engulf the place, and the curtain will be drawn on what remains of the graves. Then, Ahmad will stand tall and spit in the face of Yusuf, not because he discovered the falsity of his prophecy, but because Yusuf taught it to him.

Estrangement

His little beard trembled when he spoke. His shaggy hair scattered over the edge of his tiny head, which seemed wet, penetrated by a light that escaped from an ancient abandoned archaeological site, casting on him mysterious lines that told of an eccentric life. His face was as pale as death. The aversion in the forehead and narrowing in the shoulders, the absence of a defined neck connecting his head to his body, muscles stretched over the dead skeleton were the intensification of sadness and failure. When I spoke with him, I felt afraid and estranged.

He bent a little and then sighed. His body disappeared into darkness beneath a rectangular pit that looked like a grave. The sound of his crawling body mixed with his breath was like the wind whistling through a tree. He switched on a light hanging over his chest, then raised his head and fixed his eyes, like two buttons roaming inside large sockets. His panting became louder. He tried to speak but could not. His hand reached into the pocket of his old military jacket, pulled out a blue pipe, and took a deep puff, then raised his head again.

"O Thou Provider and All Knowing, provide for these orphans and poor ones. You know our plight; we have none but Thee."

His words echoed like a call of a weary mountain goat; his eyes that had lost their glow, bulged through his droopy eyelids like two small ambers, igniting when the air wafted.

I had a strange feeling about him. He had become one with death and the scent of graves—he even referred to his children as orphans. My feelings were mixed. I sympathized with him for a moment, but soon that feeling disappeared.

When he stretched his hand over the edge of the pit looking for the dagger, his long fingers appeared through the dirt like spider-legs, sinking into sticky clay. He picked up the small dagger, sighed, and little by little dug around the perimeter of the rectangular opening of the grave.

A voice like a hissing snake called him from outside the pit, interrupted his work, and recognized his presence in the darkness of the night.

"How far are you, Abu Ahmad? Did you reach his head? Any good news? Allah willing, it will all go well."

He did not respond to Abu Khalil. . . . He bent over his knees inside the pit and looked like a mole digging through the earth, silently, without clamor.

His dagger penetrated a yellow skull that shined like an ostrich's egg that was drowned in a bed of mud.

He stretched out his hand and picked up a piece, looked at it in the light of the lantern, and mumbled, "Allah knows best, but we will probably return empty-handed tonight."

Abu Ahmad. My father never told me much; he barked his orders at me, and I did what he asked with no objection.

Suddenly, he stopped working, looked at me and said, "Gather some wood, build a fire, and make tea. We need to have something to eat."

He handed a piece of the skull to his partner and brother, Abu Khalil, whose head was peeking through the opening of the grave, and said, "A cursed women's skull. What a hard head she has!"

He dug around the head until the skull became partially exposed, placed the dagger in the socket of one of her eyes, pulled the skull, and threw it behind his back. He then cut a small square around the same spot of the skull and looked through the grains of sand inspecting them with the light of his lamp, which began to slowly dim.

Abu Ahmad turned off the light. Trying to gather his strength, he leaned over the edge of the hole, pulled out his small pipe again, took multiple puffs while in the pit, rested a little, then went back to work. Meanwhile, his brother, Abu Khalil, fell asleep at the edge of the grave, snoring.

Abu Ahmad dug around the hands and checked the fingers of the skeleton, one by one. A shimmer of light glowed by the tip of his dagger. He picked up a small ring, turned it around, looked many times through the dirt where it was found, then looked at the top of the opening and made sure that his partner was still snoring. He slipped the ring into his pocket muttering, "Let sleep benefit you."

He continued to dig and sang loudly, frequently interrupted by a cough. "Sleep will be blamed, if the young man goes mad."

The silence was deafening. He broke it by singing a song by Um Kalthum.

"Sleep never prolongs life . . . and staying up at night doesn't shorten one's life."

The loneliness in the grave that is not his did not stop him from remembering his perpetual pain.

"Ah, only if it was the head of Um-Ahmad. . . . By Allah, I would have smashed it and grounded it into the soil to make sure that she wouldn't be born again and have to marry another idiot like me."

Suddenly a loud voice fell upon him as if calling from the sky, "What's up?

"What did Um Ahmad do to you?

"Now it is her fault?

"By Allah, even a donkey in her prime of life would not put up with you, but she does!"

I could never speak about my mother in the presence of my father. He dearly cared for her and felt that she was not getting what she deserved in life.

Abu Khalil looked at me with a faint smile that disappeared before it started—he was attempting to show empathy toward me. His voice faded as soon as he put his head down on a rock nearby, and his snoring returned.

Two copper rings appeared near the other hand. They looked in good condition. "O Allah, one for Abu Khalil and one for us. Enough to buy a pack of cigarettes," said Abu Ahmad faintly.

He coughed loudly, pulled out the pipe that flared his asthma, pulled himself together, dusted the soil off his body, and crawled out of the grave on his knees.

Abu Ahmad poked Abu Khalil who was sound asleep with the handle of his ax, and muttered, "Take your share of what the dead left us, perchance it might make you rich? Dead smoke for the living? Perhaps if you sell it, you would have enough to buy a packet of cigarettes. Come let us drink a cup of tea."

They sat close to the fire, while Abu Khalil barked orders at me. I took out two pieces of pita bread and placed them on the fire. Abu Khalil started coughing after he drank some of his tea that went down his windpipe, then he said while still coughing, "This is a Roman site, and these dead are Romans . . .

"That is what they say, Abu Ahmad, but only Allah knows!"

Abu Ahmad licked his lips savoring the taste of the tea in his mouth, and kneeled close to the fire and said, "I hear the boy Jamal say that the people who lived here were Nabataean. I don't know what Nabataean means."

Abu Khalid appeared knowledgeable, tapping his fingers on the bread that he had just picked off the fire. "Nabataeans mean glass and not gold, Abu Khalil."

Abu Ahmad showed no interest. "I do not know, but that is what he told me. He was extremely interested in the Nabataeans' glass and gold. He said that they were skilled craftsmen who enjoyed luxury and demonstrated that by taking pride in making their women's jewelry and caring for people after death."

Abu Khalil looked at Abu Ahmad in the dark, away from the light of the fire that hopelessly tried to dispel the darkness of the night and said, "They didn't actually care for their dead, but they knew that one day, there will be starving people on this land who would dig up their graves out of hunger. And because they are our ancestors, they cared about us and showed that by leaving us glass in their graves."

Abu Khalil tapped on the bread again, cut a piece, and continued. "Let us stop this guessing and show him the rings. He might discover something special about them that will raise their price to fetch more than the cost of a pack of cigarettes. He is the one who would know if it is Roman or Nabataean, as he claims."

Abu Ahmad touched his pocket feeling for the ring he stole from the grave. He placed his hand in his pocket to make sure it was there and said, "I don't give a damn if they were Nabataeans or Romans. All that I need is twenty dinars to pay the grocer."

I did not understand at the time what he said, but something stirred my conscience—made me feel closer to him. I gazed at the sky trying to figure him out but was interrupted with him kicking me with his foot, pointing at the teapot with the cup in his hand.

He did not give me the time to think about what he was saying, and take his side, not even for a moment. His behavior made me feel distant at times, and sometimes I even felt he was a stranger and all that I had in common with him was our name.

The two men fell asleep by the fire while I continued to feed it wormwood and camel dung, and wait for the sun to rise.

I then noticed a delicate inscription on a rectangular stone nearby. I tried to decipher it, but I could not. It looked to me like English letters, which is all that I knew of the English language; I could not make anything out of it, so I memorized the letters.

I wondered, "What kind of creatures inhabit these graves? Were they people like us? And if they were, what gives us the right to steal what they had? Who allows us to scatter their bones and mix them with dirt?

"Even the dead were not safe from our mischief."

These were big questions that I had no answer for, but I was confident that they were better than us. They were equal, living in similar caves, no difference between rich and poor, and no one was followed or was a follower. Who was their leader? You cannot tell. Yes. They are dead, and we are too, living in a large cesspool, committing sins, and prostituting our souls that wait for salvation—but we pretend.

Abu Khalil shouted in a thick, hoarse voice, standing petrified, with his hands on his neck.

"In the name of Allah. In the name of Allah." His voice scared me.

Despite his heavy weight, he stood up quickly, but soon dropped to the ground with his hands covering his face and saying words to ward off evil.

He calmed a little, then reached for the pot of tea that seemed empty and said, "May Allah protect us. What a terrible dream!"

Abu Khalil rested a little more, and then went to work, looking for a metal probe out of the tools they had, found one, and brought it to where they were working to look for a new grave. He then pulled a large jug of water close to the first hole they dug, pushed the probe into the ground, leaned on it to mark where he had dug, poured some water into the hole, placed the probe back, tapped it, listened, but heard nothing, and went looking for another grave with new hope.

Pain

It was painful to watch my friends at Rajm al-Sakhry school buying falafel sandwiches, juices, and chocolates, which I could not afford. Sadness ate up my heart when I thought about the meager amount in my pocket . . .

Should I buy something with it or save it for the bus fare that would take me back to my village?

I could not decide! Watching the students made me feel inferior. I resented them when they talked about their clothes, their shoes, their girlfriends, and their new cell phones. I wished at that point that I was not alive, and that the man that caused my anguish and depression was not my father. . . . But how was that his fault?

I wondered about that every time a sad feeling flooded my heart. Knowing that he had no choice and that he was trying his best brought me closer to him at times, yearning to be with him.

Yes. His fault was that he was my father, and that he had no occupation or skill other than digging graves, a grave robber. When would this end?

I was sick of it.

Why could my friends seize all these moments of joy from the passing time, and I could not?

Why couldn't I live my childhood?

Who stole it from me?

Why did I have to grow up so fast?

Why did I have to carry all that responsibility on my shoulders when I was still a child?

I asked one of my friends about his father and mother. What do they eat and drink? Do they talk to each other at home? Does his father talk to his children? To his wife? Their answers hurt me. I was glad when the painful lunch break was finally over.

The first class after that was history. I liked history—a lot. I heard that the teacher was two-faced, but I had never worked closely with him. My relationship with him was strictly within the parameters of the class.

As soon as I saw him coming through the door, I remembered the letters on the rectangular stone at al-Nakhl site, which I had memorized. I jogged my memory and wrote them on a piece of paper, then raised my hand to ask the teacher about them. He took the paper, looked at it carefully, then folded it and put it in his pocket, and said casually, "Come see me after class."

My heart was beating fast. I was anxious and worried. I had a mixed feeling about him. I could not wait for class to end, and at the same time, I was fearful about what would come next. Many questions raced through my mind, but I was able to control my fear and continue the class . . .

He went back to talking about the concept of a national state and its origin. He mentioned several national statesmen whom he considered role models, and how they gave their lives for independence, and safeguarded the state, and how they preserved its land.

The history teacher continued to move back and forth in the class like a cartoon figure. I did not understand what he said; my heart was anxiously beating. The secret of the stone and the writing on it was consuming me, and made time go agonizingly slow. The comical figure came closer, poked me with his hand, followed that with a brief smile that quickly faded, and surprised me with a question about what he was lecturing about.

"Who created independence?"

I pulled myself out of the sticky memories that haunted me, gathered my thoughts, looked at his face that seemed lifeless, conquered my fear, and said, "I don't know what independence means to know who made it happen."

He complimented me again with his yellow smile. This time, it was different. He had his reason, and it was not because I answered his question. He knew how to use his heavy hand to land a blow to my head when I did not have the right answer, but he did not.

I went back to imagining him as a cartoon figure going back and forth and went back to my miserable imagined world. It all ended by the sound of the bell, like the whistle of a train approaching the end of the line.

The history teacher looked like a manatee walking slowly toward me. He patted my back and sat next to me. The tone of his voice changed after reading the words on my paper. I understood that they were written in Latin, and that the tomb was of a famous military leader of the time.

I interrupted him, "What period are you talking about?"

"I believe that he is Roman who lived during the reign of the Nabataeans in that region. This is important."

I do not know what made me ask him about the writing. But that whetted the appetite of my greedy teacher. He became interested in talking to me, and after doing so, he asked to meet my father.

I thought about running away from school. I got myself in a jam. How could this teacher meet my father? What kind of dialogue could they have? Is my father going to accept this kind of conversation? Where would they meet? At our house, or somewhere else?

I did not want the teacher to see our humble home, my mother, my sister, and my younger brother. I did not want him to discover the secrets of our sad lives when he met my father . . .

I was overwhelmed with thoughts and worries. I wished that I had not approached him about this. With his strange insistence to meet my dad, I decided to tell my father about him and get them together.

The following evening, the meeting took place in the presence of my uncle, Abu Khalil. I did not understand what made Abu Khalil and my teacher impressed with one another. Between them seemed to be a language that I did not yet understand. I had not seen my father laugh before this time; he even insisted that the teacher dine with us. That was strange! As my teacher was leaving the house, he looked at me, smiled, and said, "Your father is something. . . . Thank you for introducing me to him."

I did not get what he said. I was torn between being pleasantly surprised and suspicious.

I snuck close to the door and listened quietly to the conversation between my father and his brother, Abu Khalil. I heard them talk about glass, Nabataeans, Romans, gold, historical value, and concepts that they had never believed in before. I heard them talk about replacing Mr. Jamal with the teacher as a consultant about what they would find, and that he might market it for them too.

My father and Abu Khalil agreed to meet following the evening call to prayer to go to the site. Their meeting with my history teacher sparked in them a determination that was not there before. As if he had enchanted them with potions and spells and made them his followers. I did not know at the time that he had told them about the price of the "glass" or "gazzaz" as Abu Khalil called it.

Gloominess

The moon was in place, timidly shining its light while small clouds caressed its pale face on that gloomy December evening. Shivering, Yusuf, my history teacher, looked at the moon after he finished relieving himself on the wall of Engineer Hassan's house before he went in. He zipped his pants and hurried into the house, not worried about the trickling drops of urine.

He entered the humble room which Khalil, my cousin, who lived in the house, thought was the center of the universe. He apologized for being late for the card game he was invited to and sat at the first mat in his path. He settled in after examining the cards of the guests playing American Spades. His sight wandered around examining the dreary house—dangling electric wires, dim light, and windows with no curtains, covered with adhesive paper.

Yusuf wondered, "Will a meaningful conversation come out of this house? How will any dialogue see the light of day when the windows are shut blind? How will this host put in place a reform program when he is unable to repair his house?"

He answered himself sarcastically, "Perhaps they are broke!"

He seemed occupied. His friends were surprised that he did not get involved in the conversation about priorities and mechanisms of reform and did not seem interested in the game they were playing.

Suddenly, Abdullah slammed his leg, bringing him out of his worries.

The conversation continued. It escalated when Engineer Hassan entered the room with a bottle of cheap 'araq and poured glasses for the assembled comrades who drank with a great appetite.*

Khalil yawned after he kicked the empty bottle away, burped, and delivered his words in chunks that seemed like quick flashing scenes from a medieval battle.

"Why can't we make this Friday, the Friday of the protection of national properties?"

Yusuf was finishing his drink. He gasped when he heard Khalil approach the subject, thinking of the copper rings that were still in his pocket . . .

He tried to control his reaction and get rid of his fear by agreeing, "Great idea, let's share this with our groups."

He said that to look in control after feeling scared of what he was planning to do. He checked the rings in his pocket and thought of all the possibilities that these strange things could bring.

Yusuf left the room for the courtyard, walked to the sink on a sidewall, turned on the faucet, but nothing came out. He heard a sound like the hissing of a snake.

"Hit it hard until the water comes out."

An old man lying down at the corner of the courtyard peered out from under a heavy blue quilt and added, "May Allah protect us from what Khalil and his comrades do."

He covered his head with the quilt again and said sarcastically, "Turn off the faucet after you wash away this dirt you drink . . . You curse America during the day, while during the night, you play American Spades and fight over which one of you will have the highest score to win its prizes!"

---

* 'Araq is a fermented alcoholic drink made with anise seeds, mostly consumed in the Levant.

He pulled the quilt back over his face while his words floated in the hallway of the dark house.

Yusuf wiped his hands on the back of his pants as he coughed. A distant voice in his mind reminded him of a date with his girlfriend at eleven. It was still early . . .

He went back and huddled on the small mat on the floor of the dreary room with its occupiers seeking to bring about government reform.

Fouad's mouth foamed; his voice rose, and his hands waved in the air—like a fan. He criticized the delay in the ability of the movements to consult and coordinate their efforts to come up with a unified plan of action. Meanwhile, Suliman, with a head loaded with 'araq, was fading in and out of this world.

"No one knows. This room that you think nothing of could turn out to be one of the most significant political spaces for the exchange of ideas in this country," whispered Yusuf, looking at the room that had nothing on the walls except a small picture of Che Guevara glued with a small piece of dough, next to a large colorful portrait of Laila Eloui, the famous Egyptian actress, almost nude.

"I don't know Laila Eloui's relationship with Guevara. Perhaps she hosted a political group, like Engineer Hassan?" Yusuf wondered sarcastically as he scratched his butt that bulged from under his tight, faded, plaid-jacket with its short sleeves and missing buttons . . .

The beady-eyed history teacher turned around after he finished awkwardly scratching his butt. Then he sat down, yawning, trying to catch the attention of the card players who had started a new game. "They say history repeats itself . . . Will socialist parties form a parliamentary government, as they did in '56?"

He said that, then stretched out his legs that were shoved into a pair of pants too small for his flesh in the direction of the circle of comrades sitting around a black blanket on the floor,† ready to start a new game. He opened his mouth to speak, and a foul smell, like a piece of skin being

† It is considered rude and disrespectful to point the sole of one's shoes or feet to where it can be seen by others seated around the room/area.

processed for tanning, spread. "Stay away for Saudi Spades . . . and deal another hand of American Spades?"

Everyone agreed despite Suliman's objection who always lost when they played the game because he did not know how to play. Fouad, like usual, went on explaining to him the rules of bidding and playing while giving him signals that would help them cheat.

"Deal," said Fouad handing the cards to Engineer Hassan . . .

The cards were dealt to the players and bidding started. Suliman three, Yusuf two, and Fouad five. Meanwhile, Hassan looked at his cards and then at Fouad's unkept hairy face and wide forehead with a bad case of acne, and said, "Will you help with a trump?"

Yusuf was surprised. He looked at his hand, calculated the total number of cards in each suite, and said to Hassan, "We are at the beginning of the game; why shouldn't we take the risk?"

"Cahoot" said Hassan staring at his cards, then in a sudden move, he threw his trump, picked up the cards from all suites, and scored a perfect score, with no losses.

The night went on occupied by this boring and nauseating game.

Grave

After two hours of constantly walking, Abu Ahmad sat with his feet under him on a volcanic rock, ignoring a small bump that was immediately under his butt. He was too tired to bother . . . He took out his blue pipe, shoved it into his mouth, and took three puffs. His breathing went back to normal.

Abu Khalil pulled a sash from the saddle of the donkey that had not settled down yet, took a small piece of jameed* out of his pocket, and placed it in his mouth, which looked like the mouth of someone over ninety. His teeth were missing. The veterans' hospital had promised to have his new teeth ready two months ago. He found a Gold Coast cigarette and stuck it in his mouth, and lit it . . .

As usual, Abu Ahmad threw his old military coat on top of an old grave and went on using the probe to check the ground looking for another one.

---

* A Bedouin Jordanian food made of dried, sour goat milk used in Jordan's national dish, mansaf, and eaten as a snack by some. The Karak region in the south of Jordan is famous for producing the best jameed in the country.

He was not happy with the grave he found in the morning, so he went on searching. He pushed the metal probe into the ground, poured water into the hole, and then pushed the probe in again. He repeated this ritual numerous times, listening carefully to the sound from the head of the probe reaching the planks of wood, a faint sound that could be heard only by the person holding the probe.

"Don't forget where last night's grave and the grave of the night before were; stay close to them." Abu Ahmad's voice came exhausted after a gasp from between the piles of dirt that were dug every night in the site of Nakhl at the small curve that stretched between the main road and the well of Abu Darj, an ancient Roman well that sat next to a long aqueduct that stretched like a tomb and was used as a watering hole for livestock.

"I hear a faint sound . . . Come and listen," shouted Abu Khalil enthusiastically.

"Allah willing, it's a grave so that we can start early." Abu Ahmad took the metal probe and stuck it in the belly of the earth which moaned with every stab and listened for its sound, tapping the top of the grave that rested there. It was an undisturbed grave, found for the first time by the metal probe that knocked on it, announcing the process of entering it without the permission of its occupant.

"I heard the six o'clock news. They said that al-Qaddafi died," announced Abu Ahmad.

Abu Khalil harshly interrupted him, "Man, he is not dead—it was his double. He is still in Libya among his followers and supporters." Then he leaned on the probe restlessly.

"We don't know what is right . . . The TV confirms his death, while the newspapers the people read deny it. And between the two, the people are spreading their own rumors," said Abu-Ahmad while jumping out of the rectangular ditch.

"Why should we care about Qaddafi? A Qaddafi dies, and a new Qaddafi takes his place the next day. Clean the dig so that we can get something done before the night is over and the sun rises," said Abu

Khalil, then sighed, gazed through the darkness, saw nothing clearly, and muttered something that Abu Ahmad who was clearing the dirt out of the ditch could not clearly hear, "This is just what we need, a history teacher to teach us patriotism. I spent thirty years in the army teaching people patriotism. And here we are, out again, continuing to teach people. Then, this fat one drops from nowhere to teach us patriotism! We spent our lifetime ploughing and ploughing . . ."

Abu Ahmad heard part of the statement and said with a panting voice, "This guy says we must protect the nation and preserve its resources. He took the rings, and Allah knows who he will be selling them to. And tomorrow he will say that it did not fetch a good price.

"You will see, Abu Khalil. I know this type of person well. They exploit people. They show good intentions first, then rob them in daylight."

He then stopped digging and took a short break resting on the handle of the shovel he was using, thought a little, and said, "What the man said is true. What we are doing is not right. It is a sin, man. It is robbery. We should not steal the country's artifacts.

"Where do these things go?

"We don't know; perhaps they will go to the Jews, in broad daylight?"

He wiped the sweat off his forehead with his sleeve and went back to clearing the dirt.

"This is the end of time, Abu Ahmad, one like this 'nobody' teaching us patriotism!

"I fought three wars in the Arab army before his mother gave birth to him. Allah willing, we will find something significant tonight, and we will see how well his patriotism will hold.

"You will see with your own eyes how much this imposter will sell us for.

"Or how much profit he will make off us. I know men."

Abu Ahmad threw the shovel out of the hole, took out his small dagger, and started searching in the dirt. He outlined the parameters and the size of the grave, took the ax out and handed it to Abu Khalil and said, "Don't misjudge the man. We have not seen his good from his evil. Let us wait till Allah favors us with his bounty, then we will judge him."

Abu Ahmad then added, "Man, no one cares about us in this godforsaken cemetery, on this lonely night, at this difficult time. The people in these graves are more merciful to you and me than the living. Neither Qaddafi nor the history teacher care—not even our government that ate our flesh and threw out our bones! It is our government that forced us to beg from the dead Romans and Nabataeans, seeking their bracelets and their 'gazzaz,' as you call it, brother.

"Yes, we beg for it, so that we can sell it and use its meager profit to take care of ourselves and feed the piles of flesh waiting till dawn for their father's gains from the dirt or the graves, or from the skulls and skeletons that he scattered around.

"This is our profession, brother. We work with the cemetery, and others make deals with everything and everyone and exploit us. Our children find nothing to eat except bread and tea, and you still talk about loyalty and belonging?

"Even Um Ahmad, no longer sees me as a real man. I have become timid even in bed. I barely sleep with her once or twice a month.

"This is not justice."

He raised his face to the sky and called in a loud voice, "I swear, I swear, if we strike it rich today, I will pleasure Um Ahmad and make her wonder what happened. This is a promise, Um Ahmad."

Ahmad took the donkey after dropping its load and tied it away from the location of the dig, at the curve that led out of the site to Khabari, in case of a police raid, in addition to the general surveillances that they routinely carried out.

The boy, who was at the threshold of manhood with raging hormones, stood at the edge of the pit listening to his uncle and his father's conversation while working together, cleaning the dirt from the grave.

He scratched himself and let his imagination soar through the dark night, lit only by Abu Ahmad's lantern, which he stretched into the dig for Abu Khalil to see where he stepped.

"How long will this death go on?" He asked himself, disgusted with everything around him.

He scratched himself again and worried, "In the daytime, I live a stranger among my classmates. At night, I scatter the bones of people on top of the soil. I have no features of my own. I started to look like these skeletons."

The boy's eyes flashed to the edge of the pit. He kneeled, put his hands between his legs, and laid his head over the small hill next to the grave, oblivious of the world around him.

A dim light broke through the darkness, slipped into his heart, and increased its beats. His mind drifted to his fingers that were fondling himself. He was fed up with his life, that seemed rotten, despite its shortness.

He imagined himself a broken-winged bird stuck in an eternal oil slick.

He pulled his hand from under his belt . . .

He rebelled against his melancholy life when his heartbeat was raised . . .

He got up quickly and walked over to the donkey that he had no use for at the start of the night, pretending to check on her, and left behind Abu Ahmad and Abu Khalil, in the ditch, dissecting the virtues of the history teacher, chewing on the night's pain, without teeth.

Honor

It was one hour before midnight. The wintry night sky was painted with a halo of colors surrounding the body of the moon that seemed different that night. The stars faded as you tracked them with your eyes—melted into the vast sky above.

Yusuf, who moved from his hometown to teach history at Rajm al-Sakhry High School, dragged his feet to his rented house near the school.

A long, dark street stretched between Yusuf's house and the house of Engineer Hassan whom he met when the engineer was fixing the school's gate. Their relationship grew stronger through their participation in the Friday marches and reform activism. Khalil admired the history teacher's eloquent and cultured speech and invited him to join them in their weekly meetings at his house, despite his appearance—his hair was unkempt, his beard untrimmed—and his repulsive habits—he frequently stuck his hand under his belt scratching his butt, which everyone found disgusting.

"I don't know why the distance seemed longer tonight," said Yusuf while reciting verses that he thought might protect him from the devil.

The black dog that followed him panting,* since he left Hassan's house, scared him.

He took out a cigarette, placed it in his mouth, lit it with a match, took two deep puffs, then stopped and watched the movement of the dog that stopped too.

He turned back, looked to his right and left. The dog disappeared, and his fear escalated. He did not feel safe. His heart was beating fast, so he hurried to his house. The house seemed far away, even though it was near.

He walked quietly to the window of the room next to his bedroom and stood there pretending that he was relieving himself while eavesdropping on the whispering in the room.

"What is she doing?

"Is she meeting her lover behind my back? I want to kill her. I, not anybody else."

He said that holding a cough that almost gave him away.

He heard a faint noise, pierced by a muffled laugh, followed by a movement of something breaking, and then a sound of something being dragged on the floor.

His fear of facing what he thought of increased. His heartbeat raced. He looked around in the darkness surrounding him and found nothing that he could use to defend himself in case he found someone in his house.

He knocked on the door in a hurry and got ready. He put his ear on the door to see if he could hear something new. Heavy footsteps dragging a body. He only heard a screech. The sound rose and slowly drew near.

Suddenly, the door opened.

His eyes widened. He did not hear her voice returning his greeting. All he could hear was his breath, like the purring of a cat in a dark well. She seemed not herself.

He did not remember that it was Friday night, and that she was waiting for him patiently. He kept forgetting that Friday night was the only night which he came near her, and sometimes without washing himself from the soils of the week. He was not used to taking baths. He

---

* Black dogs and cats are considered bad luck and a sign of the presence of evil spirits and djinn.

had a phobia about bathing since he was a child, when he was forced to do so, and sometimes beaten to make him take a bath at the end of the week.

He looked into her eyes. His suspicions became greater, and at this moment, his feeling of estrangement grew.

"Where are you going to hide him from me? I know all your tricks. I hope he is not one of my friends, cheater." He said that to himself while staring into her eyes. His behavior increasingly surprised her.

He entered the house in a hurry, searching the place with his eyes. She stood at the door, observing what was going on, perplexed, watching his actions, alert, tracing each of his bizarre movements.

She felt her throat dry, and her eyelids droop. His body that suddenly seemed small, prevented all the air in the room from reaching her.

Her hands trembled, and she felt her end near. She managed to pull herself together, took a deep breath, and closed the door. Anger was burning through her eyes, and she said sarcastically, "If you suspect me so much, why do you stay married to me?

"Don't you have honor?

"How could you suspect your wife this much, and stay married to her?

"Look into my eyes; did you find him in the bedroom?"

Her wounded questions flowed out of her dry throat. She closed the door, slipped into the bed, and huddled under the cover.

He felt guilty, tried to explain that he did not mean what she understood, and made ridiculous excuses that did not convince her.

Her stepmother's presence and her brother's cruelty were not the only reasons that prevented her from asking for a divorce from this loathsome, suspicious husband.

It was her incurable sterility that made her feel that she did not have many options, and exasperated his doubts, thinking that she could cheat on him without getting pregnant. This turned his suspicions into a clinical, uncurable condition.

Yusuf, the history teacher sat in the large chair in front of the TV and saw that it had been moved. This made him realize that she was moving his chair from one place to another, making the noise that he heard outside the door, and that he had wronged her. He placed his head between his hands and blamed his sleeping conscience.

He picked up the remote control, searched dozens of channels quickly, and aimlessly turned on Al Jazeera. It was broadcasting the program, *Their Archives and Our History*.

He threw the remote aside and listened carefully to one the guests on the program. He heard his wife, Sawsan, crying the pain and indignation that she was constantly subjected to by his suspicions, which could not be healed no matter how much he apologized.

His dreams were broken, and the image of marriage was shattered in her mind.

The world lost its sanctity, and her days seemed like bubbles that died as soon as they were formed. She continued to cry, then pulled the cover off her head and said loudly, "You've become unbearable. I cannot stand hearing your voice. I hate you; I hate you. Divorce me if you are a man."

A thunderbolt fell on his head as he was still watching *Their Archives and Our History*.

He took out a cigarette, placed its tip in his mouth, lit it, and took a deep breath. Then, he stared at the cigarette, threw it on the floor, and smashed it with his foot.

He did not say a word.

His mind was lost in oblivion. He felt that he was on the margins of the world. His rapid breathing became hot and sticky. He felt nauseous. The voice of a legendary announcer shattered his dreary silence and incited his mind to a language of revenge. It felt like he was spreading salt on his open wounds that were still bleeding.

Meanwhile, she was shaking under the cover, waiting to hear the dreadful verdict, "Divorced," which she never really wanted to hear, but she was seeking revenge for herself and some sense of dignity.

Yusuf looked around the house, feeling defeated. He looked at things with an eerie silence searching for something that could absorb his anger and gloomy sadness.

He failed to make peace with his surroundings, the walls, the corners of the house, the furniture. All looked back at him, like angry human beings.

He took off his shoes which he wore since early in the morning. A strong foul odor, like the smell of a decaying body, filled the room.

He thought carefully about a way to make up with her, ignoring the pungent smell of his feet.

He quickly walked into the bedroom, scratched his head, then scratched himself, took off his shirt and pants, and snuggled behind her, filling the bed with his body odor mixed with the smell of cheap tobacco.

He paused a little, gathered his thoughts, and whispered in a cold voice, "Sorry, my love."

He ran his fingers, which resembled two large carrots, silently through her hair. Then ran his hands down her neck and started fondling her motionless body.

She whispered in a shrill voice, "You are a strange man. I advise you to go see a psychiatrist. Do not be flattered by your friends' compliments. Your knowledge did not help refine you at all. What good is your knowledge? You need a psychiatrist. Take care of yourself before it is too late."

She said this while moving his hand that seemed cold and heavy away from touching her. She continued, "Education is not everything, and knowledge is not everything. You are still at the threshold of life and on its margins. Leave me alone. Let me sleep. Sleep is the best cure for a life of misery that being with you brought me."

Sawsan fell asleep angry. Meanwhile, Yusuf treated his wounds by rejecting her sometimes, acknowledging her sometimes, and putting her down at other times.

Impurity

To Ahmad, it seemed as if he had just returned from a battle, carrying the weight of the world on his shoulders. He carried sticks of wood he gathered on his way back to make his father and uncle believe that he was collecting wood while he was absent.

He heard the banging of the pick on the planks of wood above the coffin which was ready to be looted.

"Where have you been? Can you hear the banging of the probe? The grave is about half a meter deep. By the time you have the tea ready, your father will have uncovered it." Abu Khalil's voice sounded like the screeching of a distant locust, pulling him out of the agony that was overwhelming him, and the sense of regret that became intense after he did what he did.

He whispered to himself, "I am impure . . .*

"How can I move in the middle of the night, among the graves in this pitch darkness?"

He said this while his body slowly relaxed.

---

* The author uses a technical Islamic term, *junb*, which means *soiled by semen or bodily fluids*. It implies uncleanliness and impurity, which makes it unacceptable for a person to read verses from the Quran or recite prayers without washing and performing ablutions.

He was exhausted and felt a strong urge to sleep, but he resisted it. He lit the fire, meanwhile, the shadows and images crowded his head, and jumped around like grasshoppers. His mind churned, spitting out questions without answers, mixing them with the soiled memories, forming forbidding images.

"The sheikh says, 'If a man walks unclean, the angels will curse him with every step he takes.'

"Does this mean that I am cursed tonight? What is the way out?"

Ahmad wondered while placing the wood on the fire, "Why don't I go and bathe at the well of Abu Tabagat?

"My mother says that if you bathe at night, you will be possessed by djinn.

"I seek refuge in Allah from the accursed Satan. I will read the Holy verses so as not to lose my mind, but it is forbidden to read the Quran when we are soiled.

"What a cursed night? But, God says, 'don't curse time, because it is I.'"

He rested his elbow on the ground and basked in the warmth of his exhausted body. He resisted the desire to relax and let his body rest, but was eventually taken over by sleep, a much-needed nap.

The history teacher came to him in a dream, his face was black, and he carried a sharp blade glistening in the light of the fire.

He approached him and took a white handkerchief out of his pocket. He stretched his hand down to his khaki pants, unbuttoned and unzipped them, took out his penis, then cut it off with the blade. He picked it up with the white handkerchief, not one drop of blood came out, and then threw it in the fire, laughing disgustingly.

Ahmad's hand touched the fire. He woke up in pain, frightened by what he just saw in his dream.

He stepped away, checked his burned hand, unzipped his pants, and confirmed that what he just went through was a mere dream, and that he was still a man.

His soul felt old and wrinkled, his body lumpy, and he felt slimy inside. His head, fingers, and toes felt cold. Something strange seemed to be trying to enter his body. He resisted it. He quickly stood, aware of the strange thing that was happening to him, as if a foreign body possessed him. He felt his back bulging, and his stomach bloating, and his hands stretching. He imagined a djinn possessing his body.[†]

He tried to get rid of the imagined djinn before it devoured him and blamed himself for what he did that made him unclean. Speaking in a loud voice to ease his fears, he said, "How can I sleep while I am unclean? Thank Allah that I did not lose my mind."

He stood up, sought refuge from the accursed Satan, and walked toward the grave to join his father and uncle, and find out what they had accomplished.

Abu Khalil was moving the soil from over the planks of wood covering the coffin. He lifted the middle plank to air the coffin.

He came out of the hole crawling on his knees and continued to crawl until he got to where the fire was. They all gathered around the firepit that they continued to feed with the wood that he had gathered earlier. They took out some bread and two cans of sardines, ate them, and drank some tea. Ahmad was still unsettled by his earlier dream.

---

†   *Djinn* are supernatural creatures from early pre-Islamic Arabia and later Islamic mythology and theology with the broader meaning of *spirits* or *demons*, depending on the source.

Crisis

The rotten smell filled the room again when Yusuf lifted the cover from over his head. He pulled his short, fat body from under the cover, made a cup of coffee, placed it casually next to him, took out a cigarette, lit it, and turned on the TV.

The program, *Their Archives and Our History* was still on. The voice of the announcer continued to reach him as if it were coming from the cavity of a deep cave.

Boredom, anxiousness, and confusion consumed him.

A yellow face, like the faces of dead people, filled with fear and regret.

He heard a faint voice outside, stood up and walked toward a small opening in the door to find out who it was.

He stopped himself from thinking that it could be a lover of his wife Sawsan. His previous accusation of her and the way it turned out was still fresh in his mind.

He stretched out his trembling hand, opened the window, and looked through the opening. It was the sound of a bag carried by the wind brushing against the door. He closed the window and imagined a human figure passing by.

Where did he get the feeling that his wife's lover was the one knocking on the door? He went back and opened the window again and saw nothing.

He closed the window and went back to the couch that had taken the shape of his butt and planted himself in front of the TV. He flipped through the channels, looking for something to watch that could take him out of the misery and his late-night insomnia.

He turned on the satellite dish to view the European broadcast channels and looked for pornographic movies.

He thought that he should stop suspecting his wife and felt that he was being unfair to her but did not know how to stop.

Yusuf ruminated, silently watching the TV, while taking a deep breath from his cigarette and keeping it in his chest. He blew it out in small batches forming scattered rings, while staring with bulging eyes at a woman with a hot body stripping on the screen.

He had the urge to get in bed and get inside his wife but was worried that she would reject him again. She was probably still angry with him.

A new thought crossed his mind while watching another scene in the movie in which the prostitute that stripped in front of him was murdered. This triggered in him a desire to take revenge on the woman sleeping in his bed.

Bored, he reached out to a small library above the TV, picked up a book by Charles Johnston, *Jordan on the Edge*, turned the pages in a hurry, did not care for the content, and placed it back on the shelf.

He then reached out for another book by Ali Harb, *The Illusions of the Elite or the Criticism of the Intellectual*. He turned the pages quickly and went back to the couch that had become an extension of his body's shape and smell.

He randomly turned to page ninety-five and started reading, grabbed a small notebook and a pen, and wrote some notes in the margin of the pages. Then, he wrote down the word "crisis" at the top of the page, underlined it, and wrote next to it, "The condition of the intellectual turned to isolation, helplessness, and fragility."

He read that the Arab intellectual is a peddler of illusions as stated by Regis Dupree.

He scratched his head; the statement intrigued him. He closed the book, stared at the celling, and slowly said while shaking his head, "He is right."

He then reopened the book, and moved his eyes to the middle of the page, and wrote in his notebook, "If we understand the crisis, what is the solution?"

He underlined "the solution" and wrote next to it, "Analyzing the crisis to free the intellectual from it, to become productive."

He tried to close the circle and wrote at the bottom of the page, "What are the obstacles or the illusions?"

He placed two lines under it and wrote, "The illusion of the elite, the illusion of freedom, the illusion of identity, and the illusion of conformity."

He put the notebook aside, scratched his head while staring at the ceiling of the room, and muttered loudly, talking to himself, "The equation is very transparent. Then how far are we from implementing it?"

He closed the book, took a sip of his cold coffee, and continued to talk to himself. "What started this topic, and what connects me to this narrative? If they want to consider me an intellectual, it is their problem. In any case, I better memorize a couple of sentences that I can use tomorrow if I must speak in front of a group of intellectuals.

"Oh, intellectuals!

"By Allah I have not yet met a true intellectual. They are all opportunists, except those that have been saved by the mercy of the Lord.

"And I have not seen that mercy fall upon any of them yet. Colored faces and double standards."

He repositioned himself in the cavity of the couch that would have complained about his constant presence if it could do so. He remembered the blood pressure pill, walked to the refrigerator, and said to himself, "But Abu al-Mahrous,* all your fingers are not the same. There are honorable people who are still holding onto their principles and are not selling out regardless of the size of the problem and no matter what the price is.

"But you are not them. If you tried to set a trap for Abu Ahmad and Abu Khalil, they will catch you, sooner or later."

He opened the fridge, took the blood pressure pill in his hand, wondered a little, feeling a fear creeping into his heart, and said to himself, "Testify to Allah's oneness. What do you mean by 'they will expose you or not'? This is dangerous talk!

"Death is better than this scenario; and then, these are simple people. They will not find out.

"If those who are considered intellectuals believed your lies, how could these simple people not believe them?"

He swallowed the pill, drank a large gulp of water, and then felt something in his pocket. He put his hand in and remembered the copper rings that he took from Abu Ahmad and Abu Khalil. To please his wife, Sawsan, he washed the rings well, wrapped them in a piece of cotton, and then with gift wrap, and wrote on a small piece of paper, "Al-Afghani, Jabal al-Hussain, a special gift to the most precious love." He placed the wrapped gift above the TV. He thought, "Friday night has passed, but tomorrow should never be wasted."

He spent the night, preparing for the new act he would play on Sawsan in the morning.

---

* A temporary and lighthearted title of endearment that one gives oneself or that is given by others.

Tiredness

I am tired. I cannot work in these cold nights anymore, and in this painful darkness.

"I feel like I am suffocating, Abu Khalil.

"I feel like the world is getting small around me."

The words came out of Abu Ahmad's mouth slow, dragging themselves to Abu Khalil's ears. Abu Khalil stretched a little, pulled himself closer to the fire, and thought that Abu Ahmad did not even hide his desire to stop working that night; he casually wondered, "Aren't you afraid that they might steal your grave Abu Ahmad, and that all your work will be wasted?"

"They stole the whole country, and you are afraid that they will rob your grave. You make me laugh. Do you think if they wanted to rob it, they would consult you first? Further, today is Friday, each is sleeping in his wife's lap tonight." Abu Ahmad responded crankily.

Abu Ahmad thought about his days as a captain on the Criminal Investigation Unit and sighed deeply while thinking of the days when he was important and came and went freely, knowing how to handle a crime scene and catch a criminal. It all passed through his mind in a blink of an eye. Meanwhile, his words came out sticky, like the sound of a soldier in the Middle Ages dragging his feet through the mud. "No one is awake in the middle of the night in this graveyard except you and me.

"They are sifting through the bodies of their wives, and we are sifting through these corpses.

"We count the knuckles on their fingers, and find out which ones were already cut? We check the missing heads, and wonder where did they go? Were they chopped off in a battle? Was he a martyr? What was his name? How old was he? Who gave him a martyr's status? The ruler who deployed him to kill the people, or the people who he was sent to kill? How did the sword penetrate that skull? How come there is only one leg in this grave? Why, why, and why, until the sun rises . . .

"I suggest that we start a record of them, reopen the cemetery, and post an honor list with their names. What do you think, Abu Khalil?"

He adjusted himself and continued. "Great heads fell in this cemetery, and others, in this neighborhood; and others, on this treasury site; and others, they are snatched by the hand of their keepers, by those who pretend that they are for the government, but it goes to the friends of the government."

"Abu Ahmad, I know stories and stories. They take what they want, and we watch and cheer for the strong, and spit at the loser. Our mockery strengthens them, and they could be the winners in the next round. They only change their places and roles, but remain the same, my friend. Our homeland is what changes now—a bitter choice. They win and lose, and the nation is the one that utterly loses."

"I am worried about you, Abu Khalil. Tonight, let us take you to Um Khalil and ask her to take care of you. She is waiting for you."

He said this sarcastically with a smile on his face and continued. "They robbed this country, Abu Khalil. A year ago, I worked with one of the archaeological missions in Khirbet Inchinsh. We dug down to the designated depth, and then they asked the workers to leave. The experts completed the excavation, and then they took everything. They paid us the wages of ten days, and sent us away walking, without a ride. Who brought them to this country to steal from us? Who was with them?"

Abu Ahmad sighed angrily, as if he is taking his last breath. His chest felt tight, and his blood pressure went up. He propped himself up, took out his ancient pipe, placed it in his mouth to regulate his breathing and stimulated his lungs, and said in a wounded voice, "I have no energy or strength left. Get up; let us leave this place while we are still alive. I can only take so much, but we have to count to ten and a hundred before we sell a broken bottle, which we work long days to get to buy bread for our children!"

He stood tall, searching for air, reaching his head to the sky, as if he were asking it to rain life upon him. "Let us leave Ahmad here, guarding the grave site, and let me and you get back, get some rest, and return tomorrow, in the evening. Tonight is Friday, Abu Khalil, and tomorrow is salah, the day to pray."

"Salah! I was not aware that you pray. I also do not know that you have the strength to entertain Um Ahmad. You got old and your tool stopped working. You can barely stand. You became a scrap of the Abu Ahmad I knew. Abu Khalil said that and felt the air drying the sweat on the side of his face closest to the fire. Meanwhile, Abu Ahmad felt that all the air in the world could not fill his lungs.

Abu Khalil sat down and said in a confident voice, "Listen to this story. About a year and a half ago, Jamal took me with him. It was an American mission digging for artifacts in Khirbat Al Madhibeea'. Jamal told me that it was the first time that he saw an excavation group with more than twenty professors, all American, and all Jews. They were looking for something. He later told me that there is something called the Jewish traces in Jordan. It is true that this is a strange and new thing, but I understood, Abu Ahmad.

"I know that we might steal a bottle to buy a loaf of bread and a cup of tea. But there are those who steal a whole history with protection from the government!

"I was shocked to learn these things, Abu Ahmad. Especially when Jamal started telling me about triangles, crowns, letters, and stories that I am not familiar with, which are not there, but they try to prove that they are. They try to prove Jewish identity on our land, aided by the world, to claim their right to it."

Abu Ahmad fidgeted, uncomfortable with the conversation that was strange based on what he knew. It was like needles poking at his tired memories on this long night with the stars flickering like small torches in a dark tunnel.

Abu Khalil did not give him a chance to respond, "Come on, man. Let us go before the day breaks."

The conversation fell upon the ears of the young man like sparks of anticipation and fear.

Ahmad seemed like he was in a glass room that crashed around him. The voices intertwined in his mind, and the stars sparkled in his eyes. The whistling wind, a howling wolf, and a rustling tree, all these unexpected sounds fell upon him, and made his eardrums tremble.

Skeletons stripped of their flesh, others with their eyeballs hanging out of their sockets, and more with their military boots still on. All bombarded his sight. His eyes seemed small, droopy, tired, unable to see through all the fogginess.

His voice was tangled with the voices in his head, and his body was lost among the bodies that his imagination had conjured up. He screamed without being heard, and spoke loudly, but his words were muffled by his tight, dry throat.

"You are crazy? How could you leave me here alone? All these dead people that you scattered, their bones everywhere, will seek revenge against me after you leave."

No one heard him, as if he were screaming in a well of pain. His voice was loud, echoing in the night, but not heard by the two men leaving.

The images and fantasies clamored around him, laughing at him, while his body wasted, surrendering to the idiotic decision to leave him there.

Abu Ahmad stood up and dusted off the back of his pants and his military coat, which he wore regardless of the season. He buttoned his coat and walked with his head lowered and his body bent, while muttering in a deep scratchy voice, "When the sun comes up, leave everything. The sun will guard the site, not like the night which weakens the sight and the insight. Also, watch out for the dogs."

While Abu Ahmad was searching the sky for air to breathe, the two men walked in a hurry toward the village that was two hours away.

Ahmad's glances followed the two cruel men who left him to face his fate amid these graves, which seemed full of life, and the cemetery, which turned, after a long, silence to a city bustling with people.

The men disappeared slowly, but Ahmad felt that they were walking at the speed of light. As soon as their figures faded behind the nearby hills, Ahmad rushed to the side of the grave, and as soon as the moonlight faded, he dropped into it to make sure no one came close to him.

The dead were raised, and life started again.

Ahmad was startled watching the dead come close, and then gather around him. He tried to scream and call out to his father and uncle who left him behind. His voice was not heard. The dead suffocated him and stood around discussing what to do with him. They decided to throw him in a fresh grave. They carried him and threw him there. He begged them not to cover him with dirt, but they said in unison, "From dust to dust."

He fell unconscious in the grave.

He regained consciousness when he heard a scream over his head, coming from a skeleton, asking him to wake up and help put out the fire that was consuming the body of one of the old residents of the site.

He tried to scream, but his voice was lost within his body, "I am unclean. I am unclean. Can I participate if I am unclean?" Ahmad, standing in the grave, wondered.

The cemetery caught fire and clamored with noises and life. It grew bigger and bigger, and Ahmad imagined that it reached the sky.

The tomb's owner looked like an important religious leader, with a black scar on his skull, wearing a red hood and holding a long stick topped by a colored cross and a small Quran. His skeleton was penetrated with light, wrapped with a halo of smoke and fog.

The owner of the grave whispered in Ahmad's ear, "Why are you afraid of death? Don't you see what happens? We the believers are not afraid of our end, not like you cowards."

The young man heard a faint call to prayer coming from a distance, filling him with mixed feelings. He tried to read al-Kursi verse,* but his tongue was tied. He tried to get out of the grave, but his feet would not carry him. He stayed in the hole surrounded by the screams and wailing of women from ancient times mixed with unintelligible voices and words as if coming from a deep valley or a crowded city.

---

* The Throne is in the twenty-fifth verse of the second surah of the Quran, Al-Baqarah. It is widely memorized and recited for protection and other occasions by Muslims.

Darkness

I n the oblivion of life, Abu Ahmad ignored his painful memories, his tiredness, and his breathing interrupted by whistling, rising, and falling, like the sound of a train fading into the wind.

He stood by the door of his house, straightened his posture, conjured up some beautiful memories, and confirmed that it was Friday night. This means that Um Ahmad had washed her rounded body. He could smell the scent of Na'ma soap wafting from the edge of her sleeve. His mind was filled with a thought that he had not had for weeks.

"If I knock on the door, the sleeping bee will rise and bite off my desire." He told himself while holding the doorknob and sneaking into the house like a thief.

He took off his shoes, soiled by the dirt of the cemeteries and desecrated by the skulls of the great skeletons.

He took off his jacket that was the color of darkness, oozing with the scent of damp and slimy souls.

The trembling man haunted by a flashing dream of a fleeting moment of pleasure jumped on the tip of his toes like a cat. Through the stillness of the night in the small house, he snuggled behind Um Ahmad who seemed at that moment, a stranger to him.

She did not notice him. He moved to the right, and then to the left, but to no avail, as if he were going into a new grave, but this time, the corpse was the companion of his life and agony.

His enthusiasm faded and sadness crept into his dream.

The scent of human sweat mixed with the coldness of death resembled the smell of a corpse. Um Ahmad took a deep breath and sneezed loudly. His breathing accelerated, and his dream came back.

She lifted his hand off her and muttered in a voice that faded into snoring, "I have my period."

Her statement felt like a bullet that penetrated the top of his skull. He said nothing after that, turned his body to the other side, and was lost in a death-like sleep.

Silence

Dead people crept out of their graves like worms, the noise intensified, and the screams rose. The skeletons gathered around the dead wearing black hoods rising above their heads, carrying rolls of tanned human leather. Meanwhile, the news from the cemetery spread like fire in tinder.

Dust rose between the bones of their boney feet. Their images settled among the darkness of the cemetery, the darkness of the night, and the darkness caused by the heavy cloud of dust saturated with the moistness of their breath and the stench of cracked skin. Meanwhile, the master of the grave that Ahmad was in gathered his limbs, bent, then rose resting on his ceremonial staff, pulled himself out of the grave, and left Ahmad behind, trying with no success to get out of the grave.

The master of the grave sat, sinking in a chair of sticky mud. As soon as he lifted his head, the cemetery guards arose, waiting for his command.

The guards dragged a large skeleton in front of him that had been severely tortured. The skeleton was not allowed to speak. One of the guards spoke on his behalf, then read the verdict on behalf of the master of the grave. The guards, then, dragged the accused to a guillotine in the middle of the cemetery. The crowd gathered round. His hands were tied behind his back. He was asked to say his last will and testament. He glanced at the gathered skeletons that seemed tired of death as they awaited resurrection, gathered his breath, and said aloud, "Servants of the Lord, go on being right and sincere in fighting your enemies. This man is not a believer in the Gospel or the Quran. I know him better than you. I was with him as a child, a man, and a master. He was a bad child, a bad man, and a bad master. He lifts the Quran you see over his staff, only to trick and trap you. Remove him from power if you can, he is . . ." Before he could finish his speech, the master of the grave gave the sign to chop off his head.

The man's skull rolled down and fell at the feet of the breathless crowd.

Ahmad rubbed his eyes, took a deep breath, looked at the master's skeleton, and asked, "Why was the dead man killed?"

The great skeleton ignored Ahmad, knocked him back into the grave with his staff, and looked around trying to find the source of another commotion.

A small green cart pulled by a donkey rolled up next to the mud chair. The guard dragged out a small, yellow figure, his head bobbing, his hands trembling, and his eyes dangling out of their sockets.

The master of the cemetery looked at him with disgust and ordered the guard to announce the crime and the verdict. The guard unfolded a scroll he had in his hand and read, "He says that the devil is what we hang our sins on, individuals, groups, and nations. It is an easy explanation for everything we do not know. Our minds are absent when he is present. We failed in making change and hung it on the devil's pitchfork. Therefore, whoever insults your master, sir, must have his eyes gouged and his limbs severed."

The master of the grave smiled a fearful smile while thinking of the unknown and wondering where all the corpses will have to go to when daylight arrives.

Several dead, putting out a fire consuming an amulet on a skeleton weeping by his headstone, attracted Ahmad's attention. The skeleton was dragged in front of the master, panting.

Looking at what was left of his burning amulet, the master ordered that he be brought closer. He looked at his head that was oozing with maggots and wondered, "Why isn't he dead yet?"

The guard pulled himself up and whispered to the master, as if he wanted to be heard by others, "He defends the truth by lying, freedom by enslaving others, and justice with injustice. Thus, his head was consumed by maggots as you see. He was left wishing for death to escape life."

The master smiled, approached the guard, and whispered, "Burn him."

Ahmad raised his head from the grave inspecting the crowd of skeletons roaming around. It seemed to him that Abu Khalil and Abu Ahmad with a young boy that looked like him were among the deformed figures, unable to stand up. They were surrounded by the dead crowd, repeating with tired voices that sounded like echoes of cawing crows coming from far away, "They stole my bottles."

"They stole my vases."

"They stole my gold."

"They stole my pitcher."

"They stole my anklets."

Ahmad saw a woman carrying her skull, and jumping like a slaughtered roster, pointing to Abu Khalil, "He pulled off my head, and stepped on my womb. Not only that, but he also stole my necklace and bracelets."

She threw her pierced head to the ground, and said repeatedly with a breaking voice that echoed in Ahmad's head while he was trying to remember who she was, "Cut off his hands, cut off his hands, so that mine will return to me."

Several guards were getting ready to bring the two men and the boy before the master. The boy looked sullen and depressed. Abu Khalil was dragging his limbs that seemed freshly dismantled. Abu Ahmad pulled himself up, intensely fatigued, and looked at his hand, then at his son's face as if he were begging for his help. The boy's bones looked solid and firm—he was standing straight.

The master looked at the two men and the boy. He looked closely at the boy who seemed odd with his flesh still on his body.

He asked trying to jog his memory, "Where are you from?"

His question was lost among the voices of the chattering crowd. He delayed his verdict in the case of the grave robbers, stood up, shook the mud off his backside, and slithered into his grave like a snake holding the boy's hand and pulling him into the grave.

The skeletons' chatters continued at the entrances of their graves, while the master, inside his grave, shared with Ahmad his vision.

Ahmad fell asleep, then woke up when the rays of the sun, sneaking shyly from behind the piles of dirt covering the graves, touched his forehead.

His eyes wandered into the distance, his face pale like the faces of the dead, surrendering himself to the silence that wrapped around him. He felt the warmth of the sun sneak into the grave and realized that he was still alive.

Choking

Two small eyes lost in large sockets, surrounded by dark circles, glowed in a square face covered with fear and sadness.

Khalid, Ahmad's younger brother, fidgeted, declaring his dismay with his miserable life, "Bread and tea, bread and tea . . . Isn't it time for this to end? We are tired of even dreaming of changing this nightmare. Aren't we human? Don't we have the right to eat like the rest of mankind? Olive oil, zaatar, something else they call cheese, a couple of olives, an egg? This is not fair. This is not life—it is a slow death!"

He propped up his small figure, with limbs like a deer, against the wall, tied his plastic shoes, then stood up carrying a ball that he made from old socks, and got ready to leave the house.

Despite his sadness, he knew how to get himself out of his misery. He mingled with his friends and made himself busy all weekend long, playing his favorite game, Seven Stones.

This reality left a suffocating sensation in his mother's throat and shattered his small dreams, "This is what we have. Stop this nonsense, and let your father ask for a favor that will help you get enlisted in the military. You are getting to be a man and need to help your father. Playing with the kids does not mean that you are still a child! You are wasting your time at school. You are more than seventeen years old and still cannot read and write! What are you waiting for? Do you think that you will receive a revelation and suddenly learn to read, reciting verses of your Lord, like the Prophet, peace be upon him?

"Your teachers will not change, and neither will the notebooks that they teach from. By joining the military, you will leave this small village, and see the face of Allah through seeing his land and his people. Whoever leaves this place sees the light and prospers, the world opens up for him."

His body shuttered, as if a stream of cold air hit his face. The harsh words penetrated his body, and images whirled in his head, "Amman, cinema. No homework. No boring teachers repeating themselves every day. New friends, different life. Why not? The military will solve all my problems."

With the absence of a vision for a future, these dreams became alive. The heart beating in his skinny chest accelerated, and he said in a vengeful voice, "Your husband is the one who kills my dreams. He sleeps in the day and walks among the graves at night. I don't know how and when to talk to him."

He went back to squatting in front of the tray that reminded him of the bitterness of life, reached out for the cold cup of tea, took a sip while glancing at his mother's face. She was pulling up her heavy body from the floor, ready to answer him with a voice that sounded like a snore, "He is digging in the graves to give you the bread and tea that you don't like. Get out of this house that is not good enough for you and find a profession or a job that can help him, instead of being angry with him. He leaves looking for our livelihood, and you leave to play without thinking of the man that is desperately in need, abandoned by the institutions that he spent his life serving, looking for ways to survive in this vast cemetery of life."

He quickly stood up, and in a theatrical gesture, waved his hand, and said with laughter and a voice like a buzz, "I will join the Darak!* The Darak or nothing!"

His words faded into the wet room. He jumped up, threw the ball made of socks into the air, caught it, and walked out of the house enjoying his youth.

Ahmad walked into the house, exhausted, sat in the corner of the room, and stared at the cup of tea his mother prepared for him. He seemed different, more fearful, more accepting of others, and more friendly.

He bathed well, performed his ablutions, and hurried to catch Friday prayer at the mosque, leaving his father and mother in shock. He had never attended Friday prayer before this day, and never entered a mosque, even when someone died in the village.

The images of skeletons, gallows, and crumbling corpses of a crowd beyond his consciousness brought him back to his fear-based faith.

Ahmad knew that what he went through last night was not an ordinary thing. The young man felt that life would not be whole without faith. He came back from the mosque facing the sharp silence and a stillness that lingered behind a wall of fear. He sat squatting on the small stone wall that hid the entrance to the house and prevented stray animals from entering the house, recalling images that stuck in his memory, shattering as he continued to think about them.

---

* Part of the national security apparatus in Jordan and the first to be launched with the establishment of the Jordanian government on April 11, 1921. It was originally part of the Jordanian Army, then moved under the National Security Forces, and even operated as an independent agency for a while. Its main function is protecting Jordan's internal security related to the control of riots and terrorism and solving major disputes between tribes. It also serves as a peace-keeping force representing Jordan in international and humanitarian efforts. It depends heavily on the Jordanian tribes, especially from the south, for recruits.

Coincidence

I t was not just a coincidence; it was not even praying, and it was not the history teacher that preached nationalism and encouraged his students to join the Friday protests that led Ahmad to participate in the protest.

It was the small, strange bag in which the young man hid an ax that he took to the blacksmith to sharpen. Even though Abu Ahmad forbade Ahmad from taking part in any activities that he believed tried to break the allegiances his people made to the rulers of the nation,* Ahmad took a chance that day and participated in the march, thinking that it would please his teacher, who he believed would be there.

With the memories of the cemetery still fresh in his mind, the people coming out of the mosque seemed like skeletons. He sheltered himself against a wall that led to the street which was becoming increasingly crowded with people. The voices were rising, "The people want reform, the people want reform. The people want to topple . . ."

---

* In reference to the historical allegiance of the Jordanian tribes to the House of Hashim during the Arab Revolt, and the subsequent allegiance to Prince Abdalla, later King Abdalla I, the successive Hashemite kings that ruled, and are still ruling Jordan.

Ahmad's attention was drawn to a group of Darak ready for confrontation. He imagined his brother who could barely carry a rifle, buffed, standing with them, watching the people. He then imagined Khalid beating him up.

He pulled himself together after checking the bag one more time, and justified his decision again for himself, indulging in his innocent thoughts while looking for his history teacher in order to prove to his teacher that he was there.

The protest ended at a small platform with a few chairs and many signs and posters. A short man with a light beard, wearing a used suit and a skinny tie, stood on a small stage with large microphones.

The man started shouting, and the people repeated after him, "The people want to reform the government." The man went on repeating the same slogans. People in the crowd seemed restless. They were looking for something else.

Ahmad noticed his teacher, Yusuf, at the other end of the crowd folding a piece of paper. Yusuf took a deep breath and scratched his head when he heard the man holding the microphone calling him to the stage.

The voices settled, and the people relaxed.

The figures in the crowd looked like shadows, and the stage seemed far away. The teacher tried to gather his thoughts and jog his memory.

Ahmad, with difficulty, walked through the crowd and followed his teacher to the stage until he got close.

The teacher held the mic and repeated in a loud voice which was intended to grab the attention of the crowd and fight his fear. He started, "People want to change the system . . ."

People seemed like shadows going in and out according to the importance of what he said, "It is the will of the ruling class and not the will of the people. We must sustain a constant pressure. The regime must be aware of the King's constitutional powers."

The history teacher went on speaking about the '56 elections and the powers of the King in the parliamentary system, and about the role of radical intellectuals in shaping the identity of the movement and leading the process of transformation in the state.

He warned against leaving the field to the politicians, who built most of their decisions on immediate and personal interests.

The man, who looked like he knew the future, strongly warned that among the crowd there are elements who would try to rob the people of their will and would negotiate with the ruling class, selling them out.

Ahmad who stood there unaware of what his teacher meant, whispered to himself, "How similar is daytime to nighttime?"

He walked closer to the stage and tried to raise his head mustering a forced smile that showed his wide yellow teeth, trying to get his teacher's attention.

Engineer Hassan watched with admiration the history teacher's ability to weave the sentences together, link events, and create a vision for the days to come.

He walked toward the stage clapping for the teacher who just finished his speech, held his hand up, and whispered, "None can match you in your skills at playing cards, or playing with words. Your tongue is ten inches long."

He said it hiding a hint of admiration and respect. "Speaking to people is also a card game; get ready for tonight."

The history teacher gathered his papers, put them in his pocket, and muttered, "What do you think about my talk?"

Ahmad, walking with difficulty behind his teacher, clapped his hands. His enthusiasm faded when he recalled last night's nightmare when the teacher cut off his manly part. Ahmad looked around, then reached out and touched himself to make sure that his was still there.

Another man rose to the stage in the parade of speeches; the leaders of the movement deployed to fuel the enthusiasm of the crowd.

Ceiling

The sad moon tucked its head into a fragile pod of dark clouds, hiding, concealing its rage. Meanwhile, Abu Ahmad's dagger was tearing the face of the earth while he was trying to catch his breath.

The grave where Abu Ahmad stood had not been desecrated since the corpse of its owner was placed in it. His eyes were missing, his bowels disintegrated, and his hard bones scattered after the first harsh rainstorm had soaked the grave. He was not washed out of the grave during the storm and remained loyal to the grave that welcomed him as a fresh body, holding his pile of bones together.

Abu Ahmad did not know that the place that he was desecrating belonged to a respectable woman humiliated when placed in this old cemetery. His ax made an opening in the coffin's cover, and the soul of its occupant came out, tired and broken. She sat at the edge of the grave watching her corpse being ripped apart, listening to the snoring-like sound of Abu Ahmad breathing.

Before he made it to the head, the light of his dim lantern flashed over the edge of a glass figure huddled between the skeleton's neck and shoulders. A smile, emerging from behind the thick moustache covering Abu Ahmad's mouth, glowed over the folds of his face, proclaiming a fleeting sign of pleasure.

He pulled his back to the edge of the opening to take a deep breath and share the good news about his discovery with his brother, Abu Khalil.

His dreams swelled, his breathing became heavy, and his heartbeat accelerated. Abu Ahmad pulled the head away from the body; the soul ascended high into the clouds, and the strange figure started to slowly take shape. The image looked round; Abu Ahmad was still trying to figure out what he saw, not realizing that what he was looking at was a pitcher that was over two thousand years old.

He rubbed his face, marked by the scars of life, pain, and the traces of poverty, and was engulfed in the shadow of the harsh, dark nights with faint rays of light coming from behind the hills covering the graves that frequently echoed the screams of their occupants.

The four sides of the pitcher were revealed, each with an image of one of the kings that ruled the region.

Abu Ahmad came out and placed the pitcher over a rectangular stone close to the fire, and examined it, mumbling, "With faces, four faces, Abu Khalil. It will fetch thousands. May Allah reward us for our efforts. I swear if this pitcher pays my debt; I will stop this dirty work. I am tired, Abu Khalil, with so little pay.

"You see the world around me. There are those who have secured themselves and their children financially, and there are those who have their retirement, and others have children that will help them, or a piece of land that they may sell.* Except me. I have piles of flesh, my wife, and my children, to take care of. I am forced to work any job, day and night, to provide for them, regardless of how filthy or disgusting the job it is."

"We are all in the same boat. The lucky ones in this village are the ones who can provide bread for their children.

"The country was robbed by a small group, and most of the people are in debt to the banks."

---

* Ancestral land is a source of wealth for many Jordanians, especially after the spike in prime land prices, triggered by the continuous increase of refugees and others from neighboring countries, coming to Jordan for its stability, security, and relatively inclusive culture.

"Oh, Abu Khalil. If one of the kids is willing to work, I would place him in the army to help.

"Abu Khalil, we need to show this pitcher to Jamal, so he can appraise it. It is unusual. I have never seen anything like it. It is a fortune that we should not squander!"

They both agreed that the pitcher was of great value. Ahmad realized later that a fortune for those who dig the face of earth and create havoc on the skulls of the inhabitants of the cemeteries is barely enough to dispel their sorrows and feed their hunger.

Meanwhile, a fortune to the history teacher who waited long for such an opportunity is a different thing. It is much more for the middleman who buys the product, the one who sells his patriotism to the students during the day and exploits their parents' findings at night. Fortune is something else to those who end up with the glass vessel—it is not measured by a price, but by a homeland.

Ahmad moved away from them and sat by the mouth of the well of Abu Tabqat, ready to perform his ablutions for a prayer whose purpose and timing neither his father nor his uncle could figure out. They had grown leery of the sudden, increased devotion of the young man and the faith that grew with the growing of the hair at the edges of his small face.

Feda'i

The light that erased the darkness of the night and turned the ruins to what looked like a battlefield, made their shadows appear like spears that rose and fell when they moved up and down.

The land shrunk in Abu Khalil's eyes when he saw the light of the security forces car approach through the darkness. They rarely came without a report.

The flashing of the lights spread terror over the cemetery. Ahmad jumped like a deer running away from a spotted leopard speeding through the darkness.

Abu Khalil grabbed the glass pitcher and jumped into the next cave, which he knew like a mole that knows the landscape of the terrain despite its inability to see. Abu Ahmad's body jumped out of the grave, engulfed in darkness like a bag of hay rolling through the cracks between the rocks, holding his pipe in his hand, partially covering it while panting.

The moon was pinching the edge of the winter month that night. It slowly faded away leaving its trace on the gloomy clouds, charting its path, and telling of its pain. The land was shyly reaching out to the piles of rocks. The flimsy houses looked like ghost houses, a refuge to the souls that escaped from al-Khabary cemetery.

The old cave that guarded the memory of the ruins opened its mouth to receive its secrets and protect the downtrodden.

Abu Khalil, who jumped in the cave first, did not realize that he would be jumping into a muddy pit full of memories that took him back to the first of December after the Naksah of 1967 . . . when Israel planned the Six-Day War, and made it happen.* A play simply orchestrated on Palestinian land in which Israel was the victim and the hero, and the Arabs were the "extras."

Abu Khalil was seventeen at the time. He was not fully aware of what was happening, but he knew that something was going on. During that time, his cousin appeared in a khaki outfit with his head wrapped with a black and white keffiyeh.† He was sitting behind a machine gun in a small Land Rover, and he took Abu Khalil for a ride.

The days that followed left behind traces of barren memories. They settled there and etched their marks on Abu Khalil's mind like the scars that now covered his face.

He felt a disturbing sting like the barking of a hurried dog in the dark distance, or the sound of a chirping cockroach at a silent moment at sunset, lingering.

Those were the anxious souls that provoked the hidden spots in a fragile memory that rose and fell in the crowdedness of pain, amazement, and trepidation. They were the memories of Abu Khalil, triggered by fear.

---

* The war of June 1967, also known as the Six-Day War, in which the Egyptian, Jordanian, and Syrian forces were gravely defeated by Israel with a great number of Arab casualties. The war led to the Israeli occupation of the Sinai, the Gaza Strip, the West Bank, and the Golan Heights and opened the door to the establishment of Israeli settlements in the occupied territories.

† A traditional white and black head covering still used by Arab men, mainly in the Levant. It became the symbol of Palestinian resistance worn by men and women activists inside and outside Palestine to indicate patriotism and display defiance.

He scratched his face, lit his small lantern, and inspected the path that he knew well.

He walked into the cavity of the cave, went down a few ancient steps, Roman or perhaps Nabataean, still there embracing the moon at night and making peace with the sun in the daytime, watching visitors come in and out, reading their fortunes inside this hollow earth.

"God willing, we got away. The devils, some of them are as fast as an arrow. If they caught us, we would have been entangled in endless questions, but if they had caught others, they would have facilitated things for them."

He sat on a high rock inside the cave, took a deep breath, and looked around his lantern inspecting its light that was still pulsing silently.

The clamor of boxes, men's voices, and the coughs of soldiers, triggered his memory.

"Oh, Ahmad, my nephew. I was about your age, looking for a job after I left tending my uncle's, Abu Muhammad's, sheep. Mustapha came and took me to the ruins at night without saying a word.

"It was more like an abduction. The only thing I could hear at the time was a sound coming through the radio from the Voice of Arab radio station, songs with an Egyptian accent, some of which I did not understand.

"Mustapha left me there, at the door of the cave. I was led inside by one of them. Here at this rock sat their leader.

"He was wearing a khaki outfit and had a Kalashnikov resting on his knee.

"He was sitting on this rock I am sitting on now. He looked into my surprised eyes and startled me with a question, 'Do you know Palestine?'

"I said to him, 'I heard about it.'

"He said to me. 'I too do not know it. I only heard about it.

'All these people don't know it but heard about it. None of us stepped on its soil, but it is in our hearts all the time.'

"He turned around and asked someone to start a fire and make us some tea. He then stared at my face and said, 'Do you know about the occupying Israel?'

"I told him, I heard about it, but I didn't know it.

"He laughed like a flash of light, stood as straight as an arrow, held my hand, and took me out of the cave."

Abu Khalil sighed. The deadly darkness and brutal silence ignited his memories that had been consumed by graves and cemeteries.

He poked his head out of the cave checking for the security forces. He saw their featureless shadows rise and fall under the moonlight, and quickly returned to the cavity of the cave fearing that he was exposed by the moonlight that engulfed him and made his shadow appear like a dangling rope at the entrance of the cage.

He sat on the same rock. The moon sent down a bundle of rays that stretched from the entrance of the cave to its middle, opening a new space of dreams that was suddenly interrupted by a security officer's footsteps nearby.

Abu Khalil walked closer to Ahmad and Abu Ahmad warning them not to speak, and saying with muffled words, "They are moving further."

He continued talking while Abu Ahmad was getting suffocated by the cave's humidity, the smoke saturating the walls of the cave, and the dung of the sheep on the ground. His voice sounded like the crashing of bullets on a hard rock. He pointed to Ahmad to follow him and bring his pipe, ignoring Abu Khalil's boring talk about his memories that were fading in the darkness of the cave.

Abu Khalil followed Ahmad, ignoring Abu Ahmad who was not interested in hearing his stories again and continued to fill his ear with his commanding voice.

"The first Feda'i‡ talked to me with a speech that sounded divine. I discovered later that he was recruiting me to work for the PLO.

---

‡   Palestinian Liberation Army (PLO) member. The Arabic word means "sacrifice" or "one who sacrifices himself" and implies martyrdom. They are militants or guerrilla fighters of a nationalist orientation considered by many Palestinians to be "freedom fighters."

"I was not dreaming about that at the time. I was just thinking of a dinar, or a dinar and a half, the wages for the day, which were impossible to gain outside these dark ruins, working day and night. This was especially true when these sites became a military zone, prohibited to civilians. No one dared entering it, except with the blessings of the PLO officer planted at the checkpoint on the road, day and night.

"We talked for a long time, but I never knew who he was, or his name, which remains a mystery to this day.

"He told me, 'Just call me Abu Salah.'

"They brought the tea. We were sitting at the edge of a huge rock in a dark ruin, except for a sporadic spotlight used by the guards and operated by diesel generators and car batteries.

"He gave me a strange assignment. I was made a supervisor of serval workers in charge of cleaning the large caves to be used as armories.

"I realized that he was testing my work ethic and abilities to make up his mind to recruit me or not.

"To our amazement, we found ten small statues in this cave, the size of the palm of the hand, made of marble and gold. We also found numerous glass vases and pitchers, better than the one you have.

"If I had one of them today, I would have been one of the wealthiest people around.

"I took it all and handed it to the camp leaders.

"He announced that I was 'the best Feda'i around.'

"I did not see him after that incident. I do not know if he was transferred, killed, or ran away; or if he took the statues and treasures and disappeared. I do not know, but he was a real man, and I learned a lot from him.

"I told Mustafa this. He seemed at the time, impulsive, and did not process what I was trying to tell him.

"Oh, nephew. No one has mercy on this land. No one has mercy on this country. It is 'barley bread!'[§]

[§] An Arabic idiom used in Jordan. It implies that the thing is consumed as an alternative to wheat bread, useful but disliked.

"Imagine how many artifacts have been taken out of this site since then? O Allah. How unjust we are to ourselves, dear nephew.

"My main task later was to bring bread early in the morning from the village to the camp.

"Then we took leaflets to the surrounding villages and distributed them to several houses. Because I could read and write, the leader asked me each day to read an article or several pages to some of the new recruits who joined the cause as part of their indoctrination program.

"He called it education.

"I did not understand what was written, but I read it well.

"Mustapha recommended that I be given a stable job with a monthly salary, like guarding one of the caves at night. Then, four months later, I was assigned to light weapons training where I learned about the most important weapons used by the PLO at this site. I became one of the best at shooting, taking apart, and putting together weapons, and memorizing slogans, some of which I still remember to this day.

"The camp commander further tested me by assigning me additional tasks.

"I carried several messages to al-Aina and al-Dabka camps. This qualified me to carry out a big and final mission, which I was not aware of—to move weapons to a camp in the Jordan Valley.

"On the night of March 20, I was near al-Mashnaqa. I didn't find the men that were supposed to be waiting for me. I waited until morning. It was a different morning. It saw a real battle, one I had never seen the likes of before.

"After the battle was over, I returned with my car to the camp. The camp was in a state of celebration and faces were beaming with joy. Men accepting congratulations. It seemed that we had won.

"I didn't know at that point who we were exactly, but I did know that at least we had won."

The flows of his memories were interrupted by Abu Ahmad's voice that sounded like the hissing of a snake, "Abu Khalil. Let go of this talk. Our problem now is with these men outside. Look and see if they have left."

He poked his head, which looked like the head of a jackal, out the entrance of the cave, his shadow stretched in the moonlight. He could tell that the security men were still there looking for their share of the hidden treasures.

He went back to the cavity of the cave to continue the flow of memories and his story as a Feda'i.

Constellations

A hmad rested his head in his mother's lap, watching the stars in the sky, following some, and moving from one constellation to another. The moving stars took the color of the constellation they fell in, while others remained in their permanent positions.

His tired eyes wandered into the depth of the sky, reading the stars. His mother ran her hand through his thick, matted hair that seemed as if it had not been washed for a year. She was engulfed in a sudden sadness, searching her memories, long forgotten, reappearing like a fleeting shadow.

She was tracing memories that had faded with time. Small dreams from a tender moment, despite the heavy weight of hunger that perched over her spirit and swallowed her cries. She whispered into her memory, and conjured images that resurfaced at the dawning of a sun tormented by the wafting of eastern winds.

She stopped moving her fingers through Ahmad's hair. Time seemed to her like a small needle that went in and out of her memory as if into a thin layer of skin. Her hopes jumped like bubbles rising from the bottom of her past to quickly disappear, mysterious whispers from the past at the threshold of a mysterious future.

Ahmad raised his head and rubbed his eyes with curiosity. He asked numerous questions, like heads of needles poking at his mother's consciousness, many of which she couldn't answer. "The stars that appear at daytime, where do they go at night?

"Who changes their locations in these constellations?

"Why are the big stars demanding all the attention?"

He stopped rubbing his eyes and stared at his mother's face that looked gloomy, lost in the darkness, panting behind the mirage of memory, and he raised his innocent voice, "Who placed these stars in the sky?"

"Allah."

"Why these—not others? Why doesn't He raise us up there?"

"You will be raised after you die."

"I want to be raised while I am alive."

"Ask Allah to raise you up with the stars, and you will be one of the masters of your people."

"Where is Allah, mother? Doesn't He see our hunger? Doesn't He know of our needs? Why do we ask Him, and He doesn't answer us?"

"Allah is close by and is aware of our situation. He will break our bondage and bury our hunger."

"Mother, I am tired of praying. We need a ladder to reach these stars and poke the light of their eyes so that we can sleep in peace."

"This is what Allah wants. He wants you to draw a ladder in this darkness, climb it to the trunk of this universe, shake it, and cause the stars to fall to the ground. He wants to take out the stars that intrude into the constellations of others without the right to do so."

"Would I be able to do that?"

"Soon."

"But I am worried that when the stars get close and fall in our eyes, they will become tears that would turn into glass, like the glass of mirrors, and prevent us from seeing."

"It is the fake light of the moon, my son. Even though it could not provide us with warmth, it controls our eyes. It colors our eyes with its color, and makes the stars rise—images that rest there beside it."

Shaqelah

I know that the village looks at me with little or no interest.

"No one knows how you gained your knowledge about antiquities, Abu Khalil.

"I studied this science and learned about its origins and roots. This is not an easy thing. There are those who make fun of what I say, but this is dangerous work, Abu Khalil.

"No matter how much in need or how hungry you are, even if you cannot find bread to eat, it does not justify selling a single artifact, regardless of how little the value in your view. It might be of great value according to someone else. He could make a great deal of money out of it.

"Losing it is losing the historical opportunity to examine that artifact and its relationship to this land," said Jamal the archaeologist, while pacing the floor with his long legs; his trousers pulled up by a thin belt over his belly.

Jamal's Adam's apple went up and down as he spoke. You could almost know the words from its movement before they came out of his mouth.

Meanwhile, Abu Khalil's eyes followed the movement of Jamal going and coming between the library shelves, rich with history books, and the couch where Abu Khalil was sitting.

Jamal stopped, took out a small lens, fixed it on his eye, and looked at the pitcher that Abu Khalil took out of a black bag and handed to Jamal.

Jamal turned the pitcher around and examined it with great care, muttering, "Allah is great. This is a treasure. A great treasure that will take us back to the time of His Excellency, al-Hareth IV, who loved his people.

"One of your children brought me some antiques that seemed to be from the same location as this glass vessel. They also date back to al-Hareth IV and his wife, Shaqelah, who loved their people, not like today's leaders who take advantage of their people in daylight and steal the country's treasures at night."

The smell of books that resembled the smell of graves reached Abu Khalil's nose, tickled it, and forced a strong sneeze. He sneezed twice, sniffed the mucus coming out of his nose, and cleaned what spread on his face with the sleeve of his sheep-skin coat that was covered in dirt and the scent of graves.

Jamal's fragile figure shook with each of Abu Khalil's sneezes. He pulled the lens off his eye and slowly placed the pitcher on the coffee table, shaking.

He pulled up his pants that were much bigger than his waste, and shrieked, "This pitcher is the heritage of this nation! We have to tell the Office of Antiquities about it."

Abu Khalil rose, as if he were poked by a needle in his eye, surprised by what he heard.

He reached over, grabbed Jamal's jacket, and pulled him toward him, "The Office of Antiquities? So that they can confiscate the pitcher, right?"

"No, it's not confiscation. It is the right of the government, and you get one-fifth; I believe it is called a finder's award." Jamal said as he turned around ignoring Abu Khalil.

Sparks were coming out of Abu Khalil's eyes; he surprised Jamal with a statement stronger than what he had threatened him with before. "By

Allah, I will cut short your life and end your bloodline, and the bloodline of the Arabs that you claim to belong to, if anyone on this earth hears about this pitcher. Do you hear me? Or would you like me to repeat what I said?"

Jamal looked stunned, lost control, and backed off a little to gather his thoughts. He smiled to calm the fear that went through his body like an electric current, and murmured, "Sit down, man; let us talk quietly. I don't mean to dismiss your effort and the value of what you found."

This calmed the anger raging inside Abu Khalil who was pacing the floor of the room—standing up then throwing himself on the sofa, sipping water from a nearby cup, hoping to cool down and gather his thoughts. Jamal's earlier statements had left him distressed, as if the world were getting snatched away from him.

Jamal realized the grave impact of what he suggested, and that for Abu Khalil, it was a matter of life and death.

He glanced at Abu Khalil's face, flushed, losing its composure again, trying to catch his breath while continuing to speak, "Let me tell you a story about the Office of Antiquities that you talk about, and how some of the members of this office collaborate with the devil to steal the country and its treasures . . ."

Abu Khalil took out a cigarette, lit it, blew out the match, and threw it in the ashtray full of cigarette butts. He then raised his leg, placed it under him, and pushed his head back. After he calmed down a little, he explained, "We were working by the hour with a group of foreigners who were here on an archaeological mission at Qasr al Banat in That al-Ra's.

"We found a large tomb of a group of women, and in it, we found a priceless collection of bracelets and necklaces. Suddenly, the Director of Antiquities showed up. He took the antique jewelry and seized them, filing special paperwork, and carried them to the directorate that you talk about, nephew."

Abu Khalil fidgeted a little and continued. "The official observer that accompanied us on the dig doubted his manager. So, he went to check on the bracelets and found that they were supposed to be in a museum in Amman. He went there to check and see if they were all there.

"The man discovered a great catastrophe, sir."

Jamal seemed nervous and responded, defending himself and the institutions. "Abu Khalil, regardless of what the result was, the important thing is that these finds are the property of the country and not that of the Director or someone else. It is forbidden to take these valuables without the knowledge of the government."

Abu Khalil looked at Jamal's face. It was sad and gloomy because he knew the facts. They were either stolen or imitated. He knew how historical pieces are copied and how things get manipulated in state museums and other places.

Abu Khalil finished his statement boasting, knowing that he won the argument. He walked closer to Jamal blowing the smoke from his cigarette into Jamal's face, looking him in the eyes, and said, "We found their imitation, sir. Copies of the same pieces that we found. They used new gold, then altered it to look old. And you talk about offices, museums, and about the rewards!

"Let this be, Jamal. This is a bounty given to us by the Allah, the King of all worlds. If you or yours can be mediators, we welcome that. Other than that, this is what we dug up, and this is where we bury the matter."

Abu Khalil threw his coat over his back, picked up the bag with the glass pitcher and got up to leave. Jamal did not understand what was happening.

Jamal lowered his head, sad, and advised Abu Khalil. "Anyway, Abu Khalil, this is a rare piece with four faces of four kings. It provides information about an important period of the nation's history."

Jamal paused briefly, then continued talking, surprising Abu Khalil, "The Nabataean nation, definitely. As I mentioned before, I believe that it was produced during the nation's prosperity at the time of al-Hareth IV. It is priceless. Please don't ever give it away."

Abu Khalil, who was tired of the delirious young man, briefly looked at his face and turned around and said, "Your orders are my command, my nephew. I will place it in Um Khalil's bedroom, so that she can plant a red rose in it as a Valentine, and all my effort will be wasted . . ." He said this and pointing sarcastically to his ass, mocking Jamal's last statement about the value of the piece.

Disappointment

Abu Ahmad did not know that Yusuf planned to show up. He fell upon them like a flashing light with no previous arrangement. Abu Ahmad had a strange feeling toward the history teacher. He was later convinced that he was just a middleman, a businessman, and had nothing to do with being a teacher. He was a lowlife that devised all kinds of schemes to steal and sell artifacts.

Yusuf seemed cheerful, trying to hide the eagerness that was obvious from the look in his eyes, which penetrated the place like a spike. He sat uncomfortable, unable to bend his large heavy thighs under him on the spongy mat, as thin as paper. He moved to a large wool pillow, took out a set of blue prayer beads, and played with it nervously.

Abu Ahmad took his time, aware of Yusuf's eagerness. He turned around, turning his face away from Yusuf, and muttered, "They pretend to love their homeland, then sin and prostitute its soil at night."

A thought crossed Abu Ahmad's mind as he said that, and he thought to himself, "Aren't you one of them?"

He rubbed his face, looked at Yusuf, becoming more anxious, and silently concluded, "My circumstances are different than the circumstances of this fat man that can barely bend. My pain is different than his pain."

Abu Ahmad wanted to resist what was going through his mind and justify for himself stealing while finding it abhorrent in others. This impulse came from a standard embedded in a backward mind of the people, in which land was like one's wife; he is entitled to take what he wants from her. In his eyes, she is 'awrah*—no one other than he has the right to touch her!

He approached Yusuf, cleared his throat and spat on the floor next to him, indicating disrespect. "This ground deserves this spit, because it was unable to raise its people well."

The history teacher then realized that something was going on, and that the issue of the pitcher would not be an easy one. This did not prevent him from keeping a mental note about his dislike of Abu Ahmad. He still realized that he would be easier than Abu Khalil, but today he was being eccentric.

Yusuf tried to ask shyly, "Is it true what we heard, Abu Ahmad?"

Abu Ahmad's voice rose, asking for tea, while Abu Khalil tapped the edge of the metal door keeping insects out of Abu Ahmad's house.

Abu Khalil scratched his face that seemed swollen from the soil, saturated with death, and whispered, his eyes lifting Yusuf's figure up and tossing him away, "You are not welcome here."

The unpleasant response from Abu Khalil revealed his dismay with Jamal and the history teacher.

He left the black bag near a small pillow at the edge of the thin sponge mat, put his coat away, and looked dismissively at the history teacher. The history teacher's eyes wandered like a scout, following the movements of Abu Khalil, waiting for him to continue the conversation.

Again, Abu Khalil scratched his dry face and pointed to the bag, referring in a hoarse voice, not void of sarcasm to Jamal, "He wants to teach us patriotism. As if we are stealing from the Treasury of the Muslims.

---

* In reference to the status of women based on Hadith Nbr 1173 by Al-Tirmidhi that states, "The woman is '*awrah*, so if she comes out, Satan will look for her." Further, '*awrah* implies nakedness. The verse is used by some scholars to justify the call for veiling women and keeping them at home, accessed only by their families and husband, to prevent them from seducing others and to safeguard them from their tempting nature.

"If the government had trust in him, it would have hired him to work for its agencies, and not to do the work he does now—one day with this mission, and the next with another.

"He gathers antiques and sells them, thinking that we have not figured him out! He continues to play the role of a patriot and tries to deceive us! Doesn't he know that we were patriots before his mother gave birth to him?"

Yusuf paid closer attention noticing the growing contention between Jamal and Abu Khalil. He was quite pleased when he realized Abu Khalil's position.

He pointed to the black bag and said to Abu Khalil, "This must be your livelihood from the wasted night? May we have the pleasure of seeing it?"

Abu Khalil reached out for the bag and said, "These are goods—not antiques. Further, our night was not wasted. What we accomplished that night is work, a job that you will not see its likes again.

"If you can bring a dealer, do so and do not take your time—before tomorrow!"

He spoke with an unusual pride, as if he had the treasure of Karun,[†] as he untied the bag that held the four-faced Nabataean glass pitcher.

Yusuf's jaw dropped upon seeing the item. He recomposed himself and said smiling, "Blessed be Allah, it is truly not a waste, although I didn't mean to say that earlier."

He stretched out his hand to read the features of the pitcher that shone like a brilliant star, its light not fully reflected amid Abu Khalil's dark coat. He placed it in the palm of his hand respectfully and looked at it admiringly.

Yusuf then placed the pitcher on the floor and said to Abu Khalil and Abu Ahmad, what displeased them, "I will buy it."

[†] Referring to the treasure of Karun or Qarun, one of the children of Israel who was a minister to the pharaoh. He possessed great wealth that his people believed was endless. The story of his wealth is mentioned in the Quran. It is also referred to as Karun's Treasure, a name given to a collection of 363 valuable Lydian artifacts, dating from the seventh century BCE.

Abu Ahmad laughed sarcastically, and Abu Khalil thought of something obscene to say to Yusuf but held his tongue, and said instead, "This is beyond your means, boy! Try to talk to someone who can."

Then Abu Khalil went back to mocking what Jamal had said, "Jamal thinks that we are robbing his ancestor's land. This land is ours, we own it, and we defend it. We defended it in the past, and we will defend it in the future. No one has the right to prevent us from taking out of it what we want and selling what we want, even if we want to sell it to the monkeys."

He turned to Yusuf who was not paying attention to him but was immersed in examining the decorations and letterings engraved on the pitcher.

Abu Khalil inquired, trying to get his attention, "What does, 'archaeological awareness' mean?"

"Does it mean that the foreigners have more right to steal it from us than we do. Or are our people, who talk about honesty and archaeological awareness, brokers themselves?

"They brokered the sale of people before they brokered the sale of stones.

"This is our only opportunity. It will not come again. And you want to teach us patriotism after all our service to this country that you claim you love?"

He planted his elbow in the wool cushion next to him, sat on his side, and continued his attack on Jamal. "What if Jamal had been on military duty at the border, and it was raining and snowing and he had to prevent even the bird from touching the soil of our land, like we did!

"What if he had fought in the Battle of Karameh!‡ He probably would have felt that it was his right to tell us what to do and even censor our breathing!"

---

‡ The Battle of Karameh was a fifteen-hour military engagement between Israeli forces and the combined forces of the PLO and the Jordanian Armed Forces in the Jordanian town of Karameh on March 21, 1968, during what was called the War of Attrition. It is considered a great victory by the Arabs who prevented Israel's further expansion into Jordanian territory and was a significant loss in Israeli men and artillery.

The history teacher wanted to soften Abu Khalil's reaction, so he responded sarcastically while his eyes remained on the pitcher.

"You mean if you fought in the Battle of Karameh, you could steal from the country, Abu Khalil?"

Abu Khalil became angrier, sat straight up, and said to Yusuf, "I have a right to this country because I protected it. As for people like you, if you heard a child's toy gun, you would be so afraid, your voice would dry in your month!"

Abu Khalil backed off a little and changed his tone. "It is true that this is wrong, brother, but we want to eat bread.

"We want to send our kids to school.

"We want to become human beings.

"I want to change the metal sheet door that constantly gets rattled by the wind.

"After all our service, we are tossed away like an empty can of sardines.

"The days eat at our bodies, and no one appreciates us."

He turned his face away in desperation and added, "Man, we are heroes! In other countries, we would have been idolized, and here we cannot even find enough to eat. In other places, they would have written stories about us, and our names would have been recorded in the history books. We would have been remembered by all.

"But here, we are forgotten, and left in homes for the elderly.

"We are abandoned even by our shadows in the darkness of the nights when we work, torn by estrangement when we seek life, but can't stop the madness."

He took a deep breath, gazing between the sky and the ground, and said in a voice like the screeching of death, wondering, "You say, I steal my country? If I am stealing, what do you call what you do?"

Yusuf had the upper hand. He quickly picked up his phone and started calling his list of antique traders.

A scent of disappointment and betrayal filled the room, as if the earth felt the stabbing of treachery in its bare forehead. One could hear the sound of their pickaxes tearing the land's face, as they whispered love to her.

Abu Ahmad started feeling guilty. He watched Yusuf pacing, speaking about the importance of what the men found, making them sound as if they were associated with him, and sharing important information with a businessman about the history of the item, its description, and where it was found.

Yusuf hung up, then sat next to Abu Khalil, without paying attention to Abu Ahmad, and started whispering to him, as if he wanted to let Abu Ahmad know that he was now out of the game.

Abu Ahmad left them and went out to get some fresh air; he usually did that when smoking his pipe was not enough to calm his breathing.

He soon returned. Yusuf gave him a look, turned his eyes away from him, and started to speak.

The history teacher's plan was to get back at Jamal, who he considered his rival, and discredit him. He was eager to look equal to Jamal in the eyes of Abu Ahmad and Abu Khalil and win their trust.

He intentionally reported, "Why don't you ask Jamal, your friend, why he trusted the German mission, which included several prominent Jewish researchers?

"This mission operated in al-Madhabei' and was looking for crowns and Jewish triangles. It was sanctioned by the government.

"Didn't he know about that? Or does he only preach patriotism and the love of one's homeland to others, and consider it beyond him?"

The discussion did not concern Abu Khalil. His only interest was to get back to the conversation about the artifact. He scratched his face, which seemed pale, and said calmly, "What government are you talking about? That's assuming you are not his partner?"

Abu Ahmad interrupted them as if he had not heard their conversation, leery of their whispering, "What did the price of the pitcher reach, Abu Khalil?

"Why are you hiding the truth from me, Abu Khalil?

"Do you want to rob me in daylight, you and your friend?"

Abu Khalil replied, "This is strange talk coming from you. You have not spoken to me this way before."

Abu Ahmad calmly responded, "Not strange at all, because I know you well, Abu Khalil. When the time comes, you would sell your friends and your brother for a quarter dinar, or less."

Escape

The heart of Abu Khalil, the retired officer, trembled when he heard a loud explosion at Khirbat Nakhl that filled the cave with light and dispelled its darkness. Ahmad's legs collapsed from under him as he stood on a rock inside the old cave. Abu Ahmad waved his arms in the air as if he were drowning, with his pipe still in his mouth.

Abu Khalil stared, like a small fox waiting for its mother to return to the mouth of the cave, to see if they were discovered by the security officers that raided the site. It seemed like a fleeting moment. It was not a battle with bullets—its purpose was to light the site for the officers who used concussion bombs to scare the grave robbers.

Abu Khalil returned to the cave and traced his footsteps by the light of the flare and sat down, making fun of what was happening at the site. The cave was lit for a few minutes, and then went back to darkness after the flare burnt out.

Ahmad came near his uncle and jolted his memory with words that pricked him like needles and opened his wounds. Abu Ahmad, like always, tried to dismiss what Abu Khalil said.

Ahmad moved the lantern near Abu Khalil and said, hoping to jog his memories, "Take this lantern. Your eyes look like they are fading. They do not seem to be the only thing you are losing, Abu Khalil!"

Abu Khalil's face expressed his dismay, but his facial expressions were hardly recognizable through the darkness that covered the cave. He looked like he was dancing in the dark when he sat straight up, scratched his face, and said, "At the top, my memory is solid like steel, and in the bottom, I have the strength of a horse! I am Abu Khalil in my full power and capacity!"

Ahmad held in a laugh, and asked questions that stretched like a long string, connecting day to nighttime, and death to life. "What history, which power, and what conversation are you even talking about, when your heart flutters like a sparrow? Where is the resistance you talk about? You shook like a wet bird when the bomb exploded. What would you do if it had been live bullets, or if we were subjected to what the people are facing in the rest of the Arab world now? I believe you would go hide with the women!" The boy laughed again.

Abu Khalil wanted to hurt Ahmad to stop his ridicule. "I was and I still am! But you—you have never been, and you will never be!"

Ahmad stood by the entrance of the cave and said sarcastically, continuing to try to jog Abu Khalil's memory, "You ran away with the PLO when you were young. What about now, after you got old?"

Abu Khalil interrupted, "Yes, I ran away when I was young, but there were reasons that justified that. I stayed at al-Sa'eqa camp.[*] I was reading during that time; I can read well, but writing is harder. Things suddenly escalated in Amman and took a strange turn. For the army. and the government, it was either you are with us or you are not.[†] And for us, it was either to be or not to be."

---

[*] Also known as *al-Saeqa*. The word in Arabic means "storm" or "thunderbolt" and implies "shock troops." Also known as the Vanguard for the Popular Liberation War, it was a Palestinian Ba'athist political and military faction affiliated with the PLO. It is believed that it was created and controlled by the Syrian-led Ba'ath Party. It is no longer officially active.

[†] Referring to the PLO and the Jordanian Armed Forces conflict in 1970 when factions of the PLO openly called for taking over Jordan and using it as a front for Palestinian operations with two failed attempts on the life of King Hussein, the King of Jordan, and later the

Ahmad paid attention and listened carefully. "Who are 'you'?"

Abu Khalil looked at the young man's face, which was hard to see in the dark, and continued. "The PLO members lived at this site and other places. The government won.

"They told me to disappear, and that there would be an amnesty soon. But I refused and stuck with my group, influenced by an emotionally charged time. At that point, I was more committed to the Palestinian cause than at any other time.

"I fled to Lebanon with a group of fighters. We joined one of the camps known for Feda'i work in Beirut at the time. I was joined by several young Jordanians that fled under the pretext that Black September was a defining moment in the history of the Jordanian state. We felt that we had to side with the resistance, as we understood it, because the Jordanian government, at the time, choose to resist in its own way.

"A number of young people joined us, among them, my friend, Swailem, from 'Aridat Abad. We met in one of the tents; we got to know each other, and shared bread and miseries.

"One night, during a military exercise to test our fighting skills, we were dropped off by the sea and were asked to walk on the beach, and raise our voices in song or praises, or military chants praising al-Sa'eqa.

"When they asked us to sing, Swailem whispered in my ear that we should sing patriotic songs about resistance that said, 'Hussein,‡ come down to the plains, and we will be your cloak.'

"I did not think about the words and their implications, nor the place where they were being sung. We thought no one would ever hear us.

"We repeated, 'O Hussein, come down to the plains . . .'

---

assassination of its Prime Minister. The conflict escalated and led to what was known as the Jordanian Civil War, or Black September. It resulted in severing the ties between Jordan and the PLO, the expulsion of its leaders, and the closing of its camps in Jordan, at that time. This created a dilemma for many Jordanians involved with the PLO and other Palestinian groups.

‡ Referring to the late King Hussein of Jordan.

"Unbeknownst to us, one of the trainers was listening. We finished the exercises and went back to the camp. As soon as we arrived, the guards were ordered to put us in the camp's prison. The reason was that we sang, 'O Hussein . . .' We were in jail for more than a month without a trial because we were perceived as traitors, or slackers, or monarchists, or any accusation from any passerby without an investigation or sentence.

"One of the senior officers in the camp heard about us and decided to help us escape to Jordan. He got us out without the knowledge of the leadership, and with the help of his group, he instructed us to walk at night and to sleep during the day.

"We reached the border of Syria and wanted to cross to Jordan but realized that we could not go back because we left under the banner of al-Sa'eqa, an enemy that is still strongly despised. If we were to get caught by the security forces or the border patrol, we would be thrown into prison for years!

"We stood by the road and a Syrian truck carrying large bags, stopped for us.

"The driver asked us about our destination and how much we would pay him to get us safely into Jordan. We told him that we might be wanted by the Jordanian security forces.

"He realized that we were on the run, and that he might be able to make some good money if he were to get us there, and if we agreed to pay him in advance.

"We paid him, and he asked us to hide from the guards between the bags.

"We reached the first Jordanian checkpoint. The car stopped close to the Land Rover surrounded by soldiers. The Syrian driver came down, walked up to the officer, and whispered something in his ear.

"The soldiers walked to the truck, one from the right and another from the left.

"They searched the bags and found us. They ordered us to get down and handcuffed us. Meanwhile, the Syrian driver left us, pointing at us in an evil manner.

"The Jordanian police came and took us to prison.

"Our jailer discovered that when we fled back to Jordan, we did not flee arbitrarily. We originally left Jordan because we dreamed about getting prepared to fight at a different camp in Lebanon to liberate Palestine. And when we fled back to Jordan, we left because we were like small children, running away from danger back to the womb of their mother.

"Swailem and I got out of jail after a full year of interrogation and torture to be recruited into the Jordanian army a year later.

"Our jailers discovered that we carried no ill intentions toward Jordan; to the contrary, our good intentions are what led us back here."

His voice that was rumbling like the sound of an engine inside the cave, heard only by Ahmad and Abu Ahmad, who despised every word he heard, was interrupted by the sound of security forces sirens leaving the site. None of them knew where the cars were headed.

Court

Ahmad stood in front of the courthouse. The only thing he could think of was his uncle Abu Khalil. He wished to have him stand there, before a just judge, and be handed a fair sentence.

Ahmad was lost in the sounds and chants coming from the direction of the street by the security offices. A wave of people passed him. He walked back a little and returned to watch the site at the court that was fuming with the smoke of anger after the courthouse was burned by ex-inmates. They thought that, by burning it, they would escape punishment. Ahmad felt the pulse of pain that was running through the street. He left and walked into the old souq looking for batteries and an old bakery, which offered a bag of bread for free to anyone who could not pay for it.

The baker, in his eighties with a small frowning face and small eyes, caught his breath after opening the door of his old shop on the edge of the souq. He pulled up the heavy metal door and sat with his skinny figure on an old stack of Pepsi crates to unwrap his headcover; he looked at the young man's face.

Ahmad approached the old, tired man, who had left the demonstration after the crowd split up, following the police's tear-gas attack.

"They burned the court."

The old man looked at Ahmad's face and smiled disapprovingly.

"They burned the symbol of justice that they brag about."

The man, who was as old as the souq itself, was still coughing from the tear-gas that lingered in the area.

He did not pay attention to Ahmad and stood up on the crates to look into the shop's attic, and scolded loudly, "Say what you want and lose that frown."

"Do you have Lux batteries?"

"It is not their fault. It is the fault of those who gave them the right to beat people." He said that while coming off the crates stacked in the corner of the store, and inquisitively stared at Ahmad.

A short man with white hair and a safari outfit who came into the store heard Ahmad's request and said jokingly, "Those who search for batteries in this summer, are either shepherds or gravediggers."

Ahmad responded, smiling, "No. Gravedigger as you correctly mentioned."

"From where?"

Ahmad did not answer. The man looked like he knew and was asking to confirm. "What happened to the al-Nakhl pitcher that was found a couple of days ago?"

Ahmad smiled and headed out. The man followed him before he disappeared down the alley leading to the bakery on the north side.

He placed his hand on Ahmad's shoulder and continued to ask him frivolous questions, trying to come across as smart and experienced and interested in learning more about Ahmad. Ahmad could not understand his interest; all he could think of was his earlier question about the pitcher, which left him puzzled.

Ahmad, who was eighteen, asked himself, "How could this world orbit around a glass pitcher that his uncle, Abu Khalil, was hiding from his father. He thought about sending this man with all his questions to his uncle to figure out his deception and help his father.

Ahmad soon came back to his senses and answered the question of the short man. Assuring him that someone certainly owns the pitcher, but he did not know who he was.

The man continued following him talking about the importance of the dissident movements, the reason they were infiltrated, the attempts to destroy them from within, and about the constitutional monarchy. He was using big and flashy words, but he too wanted to be a middleman and link his rich businessmen with the glass pitcher.

Ahmad, perplexed with what was happening around him, ignored the short man with his puzzling statements, collected the bread, and left for his village in a hurry, carrying with him new clues about his father's pitcher, which his uncle was keeping under the pretense of protecting it.

Things became clear to Ahmad. He started to understand Abu Khalil's evil scheme against his father, even though they were the children of one womb and companions in hunger and misery. It was the history teacher who seduced his uncle, Abu Khalil, and convinced him to betray his brother under false pretenses. He intentionally excluded Abu Ahmad from the negotiations and discussions about the price of the pitcher in exchange for a commission that will keep him happy for a good while.

Abu Ahmad became aware of the matter and wanted to bring Abu Khalil back to doing the right thing, but his brother ignored him and went on in his relationship with the history teacher, who became, according to Abu Khalil, an important partner, especially because he spoke good English, and could negotiate with foreign customers.

Abu Ahmad was angrily watching the fancy cars that stopped in front of Abu Khalil's house, while he was absent from the scene.

He realized that he was losing. To be stabbed in the back by his own brother was a grave betrayal. His desperate mind made him think about stealing the pitcher, hiding it, then selling it himself, or perhaps killing his brother.

He decided to at least confront him.

Abu Khalil took out a cigarette from the red pack, tapped on it with his thumbnail, placed it in his mouth, and asked Abu Ahmad for a light.

Although Abu Ahmad was burning inside, he gave him a light that almost burned his heart. As usual, Abu Khalil was mentioning the names of prospective foreign buyers and citing the ridiculously low prices that they supposedly offered for the glass pitcher.

Abu Ahmad looked at his brother's face, pale like the faces of the dead, full of anger and remembered Um Ahmad's opinion about Abu Khalil; she thought that he could not be trusted. He was fighting those thoughts, worried that they would further enter his heart and turn him against his brother.

Abu Ahmad could see what was going on clearly now. Abu Khalil was exposed. He started to exercise his tyrannical and evil ways against his brother as soon as he got close to money.

Abu Ahmad tried to reach a settlement with his brother, but he rejected all solutions and closed all doors in the face of any possible agreement between them. Abu Khalil even hinted that they were not partners, and that he could offer Abu Ahmad some money after he sold the pitcher to help him with his affairs and settle his debt. He further indicated that the sale required a strong man with a strong character, and not a weak man like him. All of this to get his brother out of the game permanently.

Abu Ahmad left the gathering at his brother's house after he reached a point where he could not think of anything to do but to get rid of either the pitcher or his brother. He ignored the thought of getting rid of his brother because, even if he escaped prison, he would ruin the relationship between the two families, which he greatly cared about. He would not like that regardless of how much money he was losing.

The next day, Abu Khalil surprised his brother by severing what was left of their relationship of over six decades, full of joint hardship and suffering. He kicked him out of his house when he came to inquire about the pitcher, after telling him that the pitcher broke. Abu Ahmad left and went back to his home, placing his pipe in his mouth repeatedly, with no relief.

Dream

The strands of the cobweb quickly wrapped around the neck of Um Ahmad who was drowning in her sweat. She clung to the string, calling for her husband's help who left her hanging without hearing her cries, although he had always been there for her.

In her small grave, a vast line of black spiders extended their sickle-like legs into Um Ahmad's eyes.

She looked around and tried to free her hands, which were tied so she could not shoo off the spiders.

The spiders were reaching her, poking her eyes, while she tried to escape from the small room that shrunk to the size of her body—heavy with its shrouds. Meanwhile, Abu Ahmad was reading al-Fatihah* for the progress of her soul, then turned around and left after he wiped his hands on his face in reverence and muttered a few more prayers.

She screamed in vain, tried to stand up in vain, and tried to move away from the sharp leg-like sickles, but was unable to do so. At the edge of her grave sat her two sons, Ahmad and Khalid, crying and arranging

---

* It means "the opening" and refers to the introduction or the Opening of the Quran. It is the first chapter (surah) of the Quran and consists of seven verses that constitute a prayer for guidance, worship, and mercy of God. It plays an essential role in Islamic worship.

some stones in the mud over her grave before it dried, writing her name in the mud.

The sky became gloomy, and its face turned black, angered by the gravity of its disappointment with Abu Ahmad who watched without interfering. The ground flooded the grave with water, and Um Ahmad floated with her white shroud with the spiders following her tender body and soft eyes, ready to attack.

The sound of thunder shook the ground and pounded her door angrily. She woke up startled and opened the door to find Abu Ahmad gasping to fill his lungs with air.

Abu Ahmad walked in a hurry, absentminded, with his face drowned in sadness, fear, and bewilderment. His brother, whom he was planning to ask to take care of his children when he died, deceived him, and killed his dream on the altar of despicable greed, with no care for their bond.

The terrified wife came closer to her husband, who seemed more dead than she was coming out of her nightmare. They sat on the mat. He dropped his head on Um Ahmad's lap, laid down his body, beaten by tiredness and disappointment, and went into a deep sleep.

Um Ahmad let him rest battling her fear of the awful nightmare that she just had. She tried to go back in her mind and find an explanation for her dream, interpreting it into various scenarios of good and bad.

She checked on Abu Ahmad after a while and found his body blue and dry, like stained glass penetrated by sunrays, divided into sections, images, and cells.

She tapped his cheek, but he did not respond. Her eyes widened as she realized the luster of life had left his.

She let out a loud scream hiding the many screams that echoed through her soul and died away, like death, that entered the life at dawn.

People gather during a sudden death, trying to scare death away, but death is the most cruel, dull, and objective judge.

The faces of the people that ran quickly to Abu Ahmad's house appeared to Ahmad like stalks of wheat blown by a hot breeze, its rattle heard from afar. The images of people from a distance seemed strange, and their figures wild, as if it were the end of life, and the world was jumping to its death, just before the end. Ahmad did not understand the strange feeling that these moving images left behind. Suddenly, he felt a stab in his heart and was consumed by fear.

His small eyes followed with terror the shadows of the people around him. He did not realize that they were taking him to where bereavement poured from the cracks of disappointment, to his father's house. The place looked like an ancient god eating the flood of heads that passed through it. He stood for a moment after he got out of the bus, watching the people screaming amid silence. He heard the pain of his younger sister splash like hot blood from the throat of a slaughtered bird. His mother's only cry was still hanging in the heart of fear, ringing with cruelty, like the clamor of a bell in an old school.

Ahmad walked with shock to the house. A cry that he did not recognize settled into his consciousness. He realized that it was death. He could hear the pounding of axes and could see the skeletons that were familiar in his life. He hoped that it was not his father or mother. He hoped that the visitor was not the angel of death that consumes bodies that rush to meet him with no resistance.

Ahmad walked up to his dead father, stared at his face, looked at him with fear, and placed his hand on his forehead. It was solid like a cold rock. He laid his hand on his chest, still feeling the pounding of anguish in his still heart. He sat by his head, and people surrounding him seemed like shadows that appeared and disappeared. His father's face looked like the face of a prehistoric creature, scary, drowning in misery and death. Ahmad recalled his voice, his screams that were now silent behind his stiff lips, and remembered his glances, now hidden behind the closed eyelids.

The young man knew that the time of pain was here, and in his awareness, he felt the dagger of separation. Memories flooded his head when he saw the lock of his father's white hair and the blue pipe abandoned at the threshold of painful silence, waiting for its owner to stretch his hand and pick it up to smoke again. This all felt like whips on the back of a sinner, soaking in the pain, not screaming.

In a moment, outside the boundaries of awareness, Ahmad stood, accepting what happened, giving orders to have the body washed and wrapped to be buried by the afternoon, and not wait until the next day. Burying the dead was honoring him. He held his younger brother and sister and took them to where his frightened mother was sitting. They sat next to her like small fawns, running away from a vicious lion.

Funeral

Death interrupted Abu Khalil's dream. In his bloated face screamed the lust for money, tormented by fear. When he learned about the death of his brother, he walked to Abu Ahmad's house as if he were walking on a field of thorns. His head was crowded with ideas stinging his dreams like a hive of mountain bees. The inheritance, the pitcher, the children, Um Ahmad, the history teacher . . . Did the death of his brother mean that he lost the right to sell?

He came through the door, drew close to the outstretched body. He did not like looking at dead people with all their features and expressions. He preferred the skeletons, with no flesh, stuffed with glass and golden anklets. He approached Abu Ahmad's body while the family watched him walk in. Um Ahmad was the harshest, and the closest to seeking revenge. If it were not for the sanctity of death, she would have attacked the miserable man.

He sat near his brother's body. A tear ran out of his eyes. It was real, but the others did not believe it. He placed his hand on his forehead. A deep silence filled his heart, which almost stopped with the silence of life in Abu Ahmad's body. He had a strange feeling as if his brother were smiling at him for a moment and spitting in his face at another. His feelings about his brother's body lying there disturbed him. His thought about his brother's heavy breathing when he kicked him out of his house a little while ago, fuming. How could he kiss him goodbye now? And how could his brother ever forgive him?

He had a strange urge to go home and break the miserable pitcher, or to bring it and place it with him in his grave, or give it to his children, who were now the most deserving of it. This thought did not last for long, and the passing moments brought Abu Khalil back to his true self, ignoring all bonds and commitments.

All were silent in the presence of death. The girl came near her father's head, holding a Quran, and started reading, "Ya Seen, By the Qur'an, full of wisdom . . ."*

Ahmad noticed the history teacher among the crowd. His head moved like the pendulum of a clock, swinging among the heads of the gathered people. Ahmad felt an urge to break this despicable pendulum that appeared in his mind amid the silence and disturbed his tranquility. He turned his face away from the history teacher to avoid the feelings his presence evoked.

Time passed slowly, the hands of the clock stopped, and the sad moments weighed heavy on people's hearts. When the funeral procession began, it appeared to Ahmad that his father's body was held on a small cloud and not the shoulders of the people. He imagined his father's face smiling at him. He walked faster after the procession to catch up with it, tried to touch the edge of the coffin and participate in carrying it. His small legs could not move fast enough to keep up with the men carrying the coffin. The procession moved quickly to the cemetery. The crowd thought that the faster the procession moved, the faster the dead man could meet his Lord. They were made to believe this would please Allah, and they were urged to move fast to deliver the body. This is what the fat sheikh told Ahmad patting his slender body and looking at his skinny legs, trying to justify to him why he urged the men to move faster with the coffin.

---

* Also transliterated as Yaseen, consisting of the letters yā' and sīn which are the first letters in this, the thirty-sixth surah of the Quran. It is frequently recited by Muslim worshipers at various occasions, including funerals.

Um Ahmad let out another loud scream that traveled through the waves of dreadful silence and spread a cloud of sadness that made the hair on the body stand. Listening to his mother's scream, Ahmad felt that he had entered an old tunnel, not knowing where it might end.

Ahmad watched his younger brother walking in the middle of the crowd, disoriented. His heart ached for him; he got closer to him and embraced him.

The funeral procession ended at the edge of the grave. The people of the villages resembled yellow trees at sundown, light and darkness clouding their faces. The short, fat sheikh, with a long beard through which he constantly ran his fingers, bombarded the audience with statements he regurgitated at hundreds of graveyards and repeated upon the heads of those who were dead and alive alike. He made the audience terrified and restless listening to his talk about the horrors of the grave, stretching out his arm as if he were addressing each of them personally.

Ahmad was completely out of the scene the sheikh conjured. He was speaking to his father laying on the ground in front of him, surrounded by people, moaning, terrified by the hissing of the sheikh with the short robe. He could hear the sightless humidity creeping into his father's corpse. He could hear his father's call to the hypocritical crowd that proclaimed their love for him but could not free him from his shrouds. A crowd submissive to fear, basking in sadness and failure. A crowd that had nothing to offer a man lying on the edge of the abyss, except for the words "Amen," which they repeated without hearing what was said before it. They read Surat al-Fatihah that they were asked to repeat after the bearded sheikh, in a hurry, anxious to place the fresh corpse in the ground and leave. Ahmad tried to stop them and make them slow down with his grave silence, but they continued to rush the process. He wanted to jump in with his father and prevent them from piling the dirt into his grave. He wanted to make an opening for him to breath. They have never heard his sad wheezing . . . drowning is his throat.

Ahmad moved closer to the grave and saw them pour mud over his father's chest.[†] He almost exploded in their faces, wanting to stop them, but something tied his hands, paralyzed him, and prevented him from saying anything.

He tried to apologize to his father, but the words died on his lips. He stared into the grave, his tears pouring out tracing old paths on his sad face. He could hear his father's cries opening the face of earth like the sound of a distant horse breaking the silence around them. The sound echoed in his head like a strange nightmare.

The images of people not fully formed, walking the earth, long and wide, right before him. Swarms of skeletons and people marched in front of his eyes. He could no longer distinguish between the ordinary people and these guests from beyond. They were taking his father, to where, he did not know.

At the same time, his father's family, especially his uncle Abu Khalil, were delighted to seal the grave and prevent any light from entering.

Ahmad rubbed his head and heard people calling him to stand with his uncle in the bereavement line, greeting the mourners.

He remembered his father's glass pitcher that led to his demise and wondered with a burning sadness and fear, "Why didn't I put the glass pitcher with him in the grave?

"Why didn't I gather my mother's and young sister's tears in a small glass bottle and place them with him so that he knows when he wakes up from his sleep that we cried for him compassionately? So that it will be there protecting his bones from betrayal.

"Who knows, thousands of years from now, what would this earth be like? Someone who digs his grave might curse him for not finding anything in it. Wasn't he the one who cursed those with empty graves, and called them bankrupt?

"Wasn't he the one who fed his family from the tears of the dead, cut their faces, broke their bones, and scattered them on top of their graves naked?

---

†   Traditional Muslims bury their dead directly in the grave, without a casket.

"Wasn't he the one who read the skull of the dead and distinguished whether it was that of a man or a woman?

"What is he going to tell them now when he himself has become their companion of the grave?"

One of the men pulled Ahmad up to the line with his uncle and the rest of his relatives accepting condolences.

He stood there, falling apart, moving his heavy steps, standing in a corner near the top of the cemetery. People were running out of patience, ready to leave. Soon, he was left in the cemetery alone with his uncle, Abu Khalil, and a few of his relatives.

He returned to the grave hoping to hear a distress call, a cry, or any noise. He sat at the corner of the grave struggling with strange thoughts, to open the grave, remove the mud off his father's face . . . but he did not.

The sun went down, and Ahmad was still sitting near his father's grave waiting to hear his voice. The sun hid its face shyly behind the old houses announcing her quiet departure, and darkness crept onto the land and brought fear into Ahmad's heart. He tried to stand up to leave, but he could not. He looked at the ground around him—fear gripped his heart. A group of people were waiting for him at the gate of the cemetery. He felt that his father did not want him to leave. He tried to stay, but his fears forced him to go. He walked shyly, leaving his father, alone under the ground. He felt that his father was crying for help again, drowning in a wave of mud, his body slowly disappearing, the mud slowly covering his head. Meanwhile, Ahmad was walking slowly leaving the cemetery behind. He heard his father call but knew that he could not help. He left Abu Ahmad behind probing the earth, exploring his new grave, looking for a new story that he had not uncovered yet.

Separation

J amal sat in the corner of an ancient tomb next to Yusuf, the history teacher. The sight of Ahmad and Khalid broke Jamal's heart. Meanwhile, the history teacher was digging with a stick he had in his hand at the edge of the grave that looked like a small house leveled by an earthquake.

He leaned and said to Jamal, "This is the first grave in this cemetery."

Jamal fidgeted, placed a small head full of hair between his hands and said, "This grave dates to over two thousand years ago, just like this village. I have proof of that."

Yusuf stuck the dry stick he had in his hand into the grave and said sarcastically, "You make me want to laugh in front of this crowd. Don't you see that this grave is the grave of the ancestors of the people of this village?"

Jamal said calmly, "You might be right, but it is not the first grave."

Yusuf whispered in Jamal's ear that the cause of Abu Ahmad's death are these graves.

Jamal replied, sounding like the beat of an empty drum, "The pitcher!" He said that and turned his face away from the history teacher to avoid further conversation.

The history teacher continued scratching the face of the grave with the stick in his hand and said tactlessly, "Jamal. When are you going to leave, so that we are rid of you and your talk?"

"Soon. I will leave you the camel and all its load."* Jamal stood up while saying this, dusting the soil off his pants, and giving the impression that he was praying for the departed. He then replied unexpectedly to the history teacher whispering, "I will be leaving for Australia, but you will stay here, at this cemetery, checking its dead with the dawning of each day. Poking the eyes of its residents, and stealing the anklets of its women, the pipes of its elderly, the kohl† containers of its dames, and the joy of its youth."

The stout history teacher replied, "Wow! You talk like you are in a lecture, not a graveyard."

"Yes, I talk like I am in a lecture even when I am in a graveyard. But you have a different color and talk for different places. The daily lessons to your students are different than your talks in graveyards and negotiating the commissions you receive in the dark, betraying the country and exploiting its people."

Yusuf regained his wits and replied, "My friend, we are alike. You are leaving to beg, and I stay here and beg. We all beg!"

"Unfortunately, you are right about that." Jamal said with a tender voice.

Yusuf, with his acne-scarred face like a cemetery with open graves, responded, "To stay in the cemetery is better than to beg for salt, assuming you could find someone who would give it to you in a foreign land. To stay where there is bread and tea is better than running away to where you eat everything, but with no flavor or appetite."

Jamal tried to justify his escape and retreat. "The situation is worse

---

* An Arabic idiom that implies leaving everything behind.

† Black powdery eye makeup that dates to the predynastic period (3100 BCE) made from galena, an ore which is essentially lead sulfide. It is still used in Middle Eastern, South Asian, and North African traditional societies. It is believed that Prophet Muhammad (PBUH) used Ithmid kohl and recommended it to his people.

than bread and tea—sordid poverty in everything! Don't you see that all of us are in a state of poverty? Poverty in politics, poverty in awareness, poverty in culture, poverty in creativity, poverty in achievement, such a poor state that it does not even amount to a meal of bread and tea!

"We know who wanted us to be like this. It looks like our talk about our circumstances in this country is also poor, merely bread and tea.

"You will not find answers, Yusuf, if you are in this graveyard. Therefore, I am getting out, leaving this cemetery, and leaving you with Abu Khalil living on bread and tea."

Jamal continued, "Don't forget Abu Ahmad's poor children, who do not even get bread and tea from the price of the pitcher, and that it is their father's right after all. I heard recently that it was sold for a huge price—something you didn't even dream of!

"No, I promise you, my friend. He didn't get the wager of his efforts," Yusuf said as he approached the receiving line.

Jamal looked at him sarcastically and said, "I know that nothing will fill your belly but this dust. Man, why don't you learn from the graveyards that you have lived your life in, you and Abu Khalil? Let Abu Ahmad be a lesson for the both of you."

They stood together, sharing their condolences with Ahmad, Abu Khalil, and the rest of the family, then left the cemetery together. The history teacher said goodbye to Jamal never to see him again. Jamal walked into the alley leading to his house to get ready to leave for Australia as an immigrant. Ahmad disappeared behind the cemetery wall on his way to his house in the middle of the village after a day full of sadness, fear, and mixed feelings.

Yusuf's wife did not pay him any attention when he came home soaked in sweat and odors. He felt like a soggy bag of hay on a couch in the corner of the house, weaker than a spider's web. He asked his wife, Sawsan, to make him a cup of tea. She pretended not to hear him. Questions crowded his head about this lady who seemed like a wounded lioness, roaring but not able to change her circumstances.

She was gone for a little while and returned with a cup of tea and placed it in front of him without paying him any attention and went back to watching television. He could see anger in her eyes. He thought about jumping on her body. He imagined her as a white duck; her sides moved as she moved. She saw him stealing a look at her full chest, pouring out of the folds of her clothes.

He turned his face away from her a little and looked around. Things looked to him ugly and void of life, except for her. He thought about shrinking in his chair and waiting for death or standing up and getting rid of this woman whose rejection made him more depressed.

He felt deep sadness exhausting his body. He wanted to get himself out of all of this, so he got up slowly and came close to her body that was drowning in silence. He stretched out his hand to touch her. She moved away, looked at him contemptuously, and sighed deeply.

He faced her rebellion with a cold question. "What do you want?"

The answer hardened on her lips, and at the same time, she recalled the painful memories that he sowed in her wounds, growing more each day.

He rephrased his question more sarcastically and provocatively. "Will you get in bed with me, my beautiful lady?"

He wanted to close the door of contention, for even an hour, half an hour, or minutes, to kill the desire that was pounding his head like bullets.

She did not pay him any attention, but he was emboldened and held her hand and pulled her to their bedroom. Their bed was brutal and fearful in her sight, a coffin, too small for both their bodies. He saw it as a stage for the fleeting moment that lust flared up in his body.

She looked at his face as he sat her on the edge of the bed and said, "Do you see me with you?"

He closed his eyes and imagined his girlfriend, the wife of the intelligence officer that drowned his heart in a terrifying spiral of honey.

He opened his eyes and saw her face that was a hundred times prettier than his lover's face. "Isn't it time for you to stop toying with my heart?"

"And you, isn't it time for you to stop breaking my heart, hurting my feelings, and calling me stupid, when you are the stupid one? Isn't it time for you to stop the way you deceive me and others, pretending to be innocent, when you are the most sinful? Isn't it time?"

He placed his hand on her mouth that seemed to him like two halves of a ripe strawberry and stopped her from talking.

With a translucent silence, he said, "Isn't it time . . . isn't it time? I do not want us to start a trial. Let us listen to the call of our flesh for now."

He stood in front of her and took off his clothes. A foul odor spread. He approached her a little, then blew out a small candle timidly lit, spreading its anguish into the place.

A couple of minutes after the candle was put out, his body was lost in darkness looking for the switches to turn on the light again.

Sawsan was in more pain and anguish from sleeping with this filthy man who continued to defile her whenever he found himself loaded with lust and desire, under the pretext of a marriage based on suspicion and jealousy.

She felt a chill and nausea spread through her body, but slowly rose and pulled herself together. She covered her young bright body and tied her long hair. Her breath accelerated by the fear that she might carry in her womb the dirt of this rat, who lay on his back after spreading his lust on her, with no regard for her feelings or her pain.

In a moment of distress and frightening silence, she felt that she was suffocating, looked at his body that appeared like the body of a gorilla, tired of running. She remembered her mean sister-in-law and cursed her bad luck. She was like a little girl, injured, orphaned, her heart broken by ambiguity, and doubt about what the future would bring.

The questions in her head were looking for answers. Her mind, flooded with memories, trying to hide the disfigured images, chopped dreams, and broken feelings.

She carried her fear with her and sat near him watching television again. A flood of tears filled her eyes—he did not notice.

Yusuf flipped through the channels and clicked on a channel that he knew well and stopped at a pornographic scene. He watched with amazement, not paying attention to her. Meanwhile, she was withering in the deep night like a drop of black ink falling out of a pen in the darkness of a rainy night.

Darak

Khalid, the young brother, was fragile and unaware of what was going on around him. His mother's conversation about helping his father filled the back of his little head that looked like the back of a turtle. The words came down like water droplets that fell in a constant pattern on a mud pile, making noise without being seen.

Khalid sat by the stone wall surrounding his house. The sheet-metal door rattled with every passing wind, warning of a harsh winter, reminding him of the absence of his father whom he dearly missed. He was careful to go to the cemetery often. He had made up his mind to keep talking to his father, even if he was dead. He walked aimlessly, reached the cemetery, entered with a quietness mixed with fear. He first stood at the edge of the cemetery's low wall, recited al-Fatihah and a couple of other verses from the Quran and walked between the graves to where his father was laid to rest. He imagined the people beneath the headstones, rising, greeting him, some weeping, others asking about their families, some starving, and others tending to their wounds. He watched, terror seeping through his side and penetrating his heart. He wanted to answer their questions, but he stopped himself. He walked faster until he got to his father's grave. He sat next to him, wanted to be around him, and moved even closer looking for refuge in his presence.

Khalid, who was about seventeen years old, looked around and thought of the sayings he heard about the brutality of the grave's torment and wondered naively and with sadness about the conditions of the dead. He wanted to ask his father, but he did not. He placed his right hand on the grave marker and drew closer. He felt a sticky coldness penetrate his body. His limbs felt heavy, his body numbed, and his small eyes—smaller from crying—drooped. He fell asleep beside the grave.

Abu Ahmad appeared with his white angelic clothes, shaved, with no headcover, walking amid an aura of light. He walked to his son and sat on the other grave marker. Khalid was surprised and started asking him silly questions about the torment of the grave.

Abu Ahmad interrupted him and ordered him to listen. "If you do not stand up to them, they will eat you and your siblings alive. I do not want you to be weak anymore. You must choose your life at this point. Do not let Abu Khalil control your life. Your heart is consuming me. Go wherever you want. Watch out for your brother, but do not stand in his way. Lift the sadness off your mother's heart."

The boy woke up to the sound of barking dogs fighting. They tracked his scent and approached him, hoping to find a carcass or corpse to feed on. He looked around for his father to protect him but could not find him. The tentacles of fear penetrated his body. He stood up and left the graveyard hurriedly. The graves were still pressing their weight on the chest of the cemetery, while its occupants were moaning without voices.

His father's words pierced his mind like a needle, in and out. By the time he arrived at his house, Khalid had decided to join the Darak.

Um Ahmad's voice was like an echo coming from a faraway wadi, dripping with pain and fear. She said, "I was looking for you."

The boy's face was like the dry skin of a dead corpse, his tears fell, running over the scars of fear and dismay on his small face. He said as he took off his mud-covered shoes, "I was visiting my father."

His words stung like a whip. It touched his mother's heart, that was dripping pain like a winter snow.

Her worries diminished when Khalid sat on the small sponge mat in front of her with a calmness in his heart. "What did he say to you?"

Khalid took a deep breath and sent a long sigh into the darkness of the night and said with a smile on his face, "He is sending you his greetings."

Her heart shuddered, and small lines that looked like swarms of ants spread over her face. She wanted to believe what he said, but something tugged on her heart, and brought her back to her senses. "May Allah's mercy be on his soul. He never leaves my mind."

"I saw him in a beautiful robe. He asked me to join the Darak. Yes. He said to me, "Go where your heart takes you." I told you a while ago, before he died, that I wanted to join the Darak. What do you think?"

Her face dropped and her eyes were covered with tears. She put her head down and murmured in a low voice, "May Allah and Ali be with you, my beloved son."

She was silent for a while, then added, "Don't you want to finish your studies?"

He let out a painful laugh, sighed, gathered his body that was spread out on the thin sponge mat, looked at his mother's face and said, "Education, Um Ahmad? Isn't that a waste of time, mother? What education do you talk about? About a school that not one of its students passed the high school national exam this year!

"What education are you talking about?

"Do we have the money to pay for private English and math lessons? And if I passed, do you think that people like me can get into university?"

He stretched his body on the thin mat and added, "The best education is to leave education for those who can afford education."

Um Ahmad sighed and mumbled, "As you say, the Darak is better. Later you will be able to build your own house and get married.

Anyhow, it does not matter. Those who study join the army in the end. It's better to sign up now.

"Look at your father. He retired when he was thirty-five years old, still in the prime of his youth."

Khalid muttered sarcastically with pain in his voice, "To dig graves, sell old glass, and look for commission on everything?"

Um Ahmad heard his hurtful words and wanted to say something to defend her dead husband. "He had to—his retirement was not enough to bring bread and tea for the family. He believed that the land he served in his youth would protect him in his need and old age."

Khalid and his mother were drowned in a dreary silence.

Meanwhile, his brother Ahmad was listening to loud voices coming from his uncle's house. This convinced Ahmad that the pitcher was still there, and that the history teacher was still bargaining with his uncle over his father's treasure.

Ahmad walked closer to the front door of Abu Khalil's house. He was able to confirm that the discussion was with big dealers about the price of the pitcher. This was corroborated by the fancy cars parked outside his uncle's humble house.

Ahmad was determined to get back what was his father's. He met his uncle the next day, but his uncle lied and told him that the pitcher was sold, and that his father already received his share from the sale of the artifact.

Ahmad thought about killing his uncle and getting rid of him. Then he thought about committing suicide and writing a letter implicating his uncle in his death and sending him to jail to spend the rest of his life there.

In the end, Ahmad realized that he would not be able to get what was his from this man who had no qualms about selling out his brother at the first opportunity, and for the best price.

Loud knocks on the outside gate of the house broke the morning stillness. Ahmad saw a man through the metal gate that stopped stray animals, a stranger. As he came closer, he realized that the man looked familiar—the short, fat sheikh with the red beard.*

Ahmad hurried back into the house, which was not usual for him, asked his little sister to go to the other room and quickly tidied the mats on the floor and went out to welcome his guest.

The man with the round face and long beard entered and choose a prominent place in the room to sit. He was introduced to Ahmad's mother, and she left after that.

The sheikh's eyes were searching the room assessing the condition of its people. He seemed to know a lot about Ahmad's father, including the recent story of the pitcher. He chose the right time to infiltrate Ahmad's heart and lead him to where he wanted him to go.

The sheikh started his conversation talking about true friendship, then started speaking against his uncle Abu Khalil.

He offered Ahmad a sum of money, but Ahmad refused. Ahmad told him that he wanted to eat with the sweat of his brow, like his father used to say.

He asked the sheikh for an opportunity to work, regardless of the circumstances. The sheikh then was certain that the prey was moving closer to the trap.

He retold Ahmad some of the stories that confirmed the strength of his faith and morality, and touched his heart and senses, taking him far away from this small concrete room that was devoid of everything.

They agreed to meet the next day at the western mosque after evening prayer.

His mother, broken and distressed by her sadness, was not the best judge of character. But at that moment, her heart was on fire with apprehension and concern. She looked through the window at the man's face, bursting with flesh, and her worries and fear escalated.

She went out, which she did not typically do, and looked again at the face of this strange man that came to their humble house, without a previous arrangement, trying to figure out the secret behind his visit.

---

* Ultra-conservative men in Muslim societies dye their beards with henna, a red plant-based dye that they believe was used by Prophet Muhammad (PBUH).

She squatted by the side of the door, waiting for him to leave the courtyard so that she could ask Ahmad about the surprise visit of the strange sheikh, who entered her wounded house, unannounced. Who was he? And what did he want?

The man left wobbling, fixing his large scarf that loosely covered his head and shoulders without an iqal,[†] reciting to himself verses of the Quran, and lowering his gaze with intensity, implying a strict faith.

Um Ahmad fixed her sight on the big backside of the sheikh leaving and compared it to the skinny body of her son, with legs that looked like a small deer that was just born.

Her lips formed a faint, distance smile, out of place. She then sighed, and said with a hoarse voice, "Praised be to Allah, who allotted people their fortunes and brains."

Ahmad stood up waving to his guest until he disappeared in the cold day. Then he returned to his mother who showered him with questions that his small brain could not process.

His mother sat straight and dumped a heavy load on his shoulders when she told him that he was now responsible for his siblings. She said that this man was not to be trusted, despite his apparent religiosity, and that his secrecy was scary and suspicious.

Ahmad's young heart hung in a place of fear and suspicion. He was looking in his limited circle for a role model to follow.

A voice inside him insisted that the sheikh was the closest to what he was looking for. He was the most moderate and the closest to Allah. He would not betray his friend and would not take him lightly. He listened to him on Fridays, calling for morality and faith to straighten behavior. He believed the sheikh, recalling his disappointment with his uncle and the state of poverty and despair that his family and he were in.

Ahmad went to his mother and shared his opinion with her. This did not stop her from sharing her concerns about the short, broad-shouldered, fat sheikh.

---

†   Heavy cloth ring, usually made of black rope, placed over the traditional keffiyeh—headscarf—that men wear in traditional Arab communities. Wearing the headscarf as a loose triangle covering the head and the shoulders without the iqal implies a strict believer, similar to growing a longer beard.

Ahmad could not stop thinking about the upcoming meeting, sharing the stories he heard, and recalling his father's dreams that disappeared in the graveyards. He wanted to quickly jump into his new life to take revenge on his uncle, who turned more yellow, after all these years. He wanted to create for himself a new status in this dirty world. His head was bombarded with thousands of thoughts, quickly whistling in his heart, announcing his departure from his current life, but he did not know to where.

His mother stood over his head carrying a dish with small embers, a small piece of alum inside each of them. Um Ahmad blew on the embers, and the alum opened, each forming a deformed human figure. Um Ahmad rejoiced, because according to her reading, whoever infected her son Ahmad with envy and an evil eye had been exposed and their ugly features revealed by her embers and alum. Meanwhile, Ahmad was basking in deep sleep.

The next day, Ahmad and the sheikh sat in the corner of the mosque, pretending to be reading the Quran and discussing issues of faith.

The sheikh moved closer to Ahmad after the worshipers left the mosque and whispered to him, "Your mission is dangerous, and confidentiality is its basis and essence. I do not want anyone to know what you do, not even your mother. She shouldn't know."

Ahmad's heart trembled. It became clear to him that the man who came out of nowhere was getting him entangled in something ominous. Ahmad ignored the many questions that crossed his mind. He was consumed with a desire to prove to himself and to his uncle that he was a man who could carry out difficult tasks, and become wealthy, regardless of the cost.

Ahmad placed his hand in the sheikh's hand, and the sheikh ordered him to read al-Fatihah sealing their agreement that there would be no betrayal or hesitation, and that the contract was signed before Allah, and Allah Himself was the witness.

The sheikh turned his face to the door nervously when he heard it open slowly. He looked back at Ahmad and wanted to plant the seeds of fear in his small heart, too small for the sheikh's big dreams. He said in a low voice, "It is true that our covenant is with Allah, but you will never be far away, regardless of where you would hide. Don't ever think about betraying us or revealing any of our secrets."

The vigilant sheikh stood in haste, snuck over to the door, and checked the entrance. He then returned to Ahmad, who was still in his place, patted him on the back, stared into his eyes, and said, "Don't worry about anything. I am with you. I will not let you down at all. Just be careful and be a man at the same time. Do not let suspicion and fear enter your heart. From now on, I want your heart to be like steel, and your decision as sharp as the edge of a sword. Do not hesitate. If you decide to cut off someone's head, only move your hand and follow your heart."

The sheikh wanted to plant in Ahmad's young mind his ideas and belief and see them grow and develop with time.

The sheikh then sat on his knees across from Ahmad, pulled his hand down his beard that moved with every word he said, and stretched his hand into a small black bag and pulled out a white envelope. He opened Ahmad's small hand and closed it on the envelope while his eyes surveyed the mosque, its windows, and its doors. He wanted to test the ability of the unexperienced young man.

He said to Ahmad while looking into his eyes, and placing a sum of money on the envelope, "Take this envelope. I want you to deliver it to this address in Amman. This money is for you. Make sure not to go to the wrong address. Do this tomorrow, and we can meet the day after tomorrow at al-Mazar Mosque, agreed?"

The boy, full of apprehension and worry, nodded his head, stood up, and stuck the money in his pants pocket, and then stuffed the envelope in his other pocket, and left after bidding farewell to the sheikh.

The sheikh walked to the window of the mosque and followed the boy with his eyes. The boy walked toward the unknown as if the world were watching him.

Desert

The date of Ahmad's departure to Amman coincided with the date of his younger brother joining the Darak. Khalid had completed all the necessary tests, and the next day was the day for him to start training.

The two young men went together to Amman. They crossed the arid desert that had nothing in it but the asphalt road that grew wider as they drew closer to the city. Ahmad was watching with his small eyes sunk in sadness and tenderness, checking the train stations of the old Hejaz Railroad. He thought of that cold night when he accompanied his father, Abu Khalil, the history teacher, and a group of young men on a dig near one of the old stations that appeared on the face of earth like a "remnant of a tattoo on the back of the palm of the hand."*

He remembered how his father would observe the tracks of a Turkish bullet that was still embedded deep in the Hejaz wooden railroads, and how his Turkish friend guided them to the place of the treasure that his grandfather, an officer at the time of Arab Revolt,

---

* A verse from a famous poem by Tarfa ibn al-Abd, a sixth-century Bahraini poet and one of the seven poets of the most celebrated anthology of ancient Arabic poetry, known as the *Mu'allaqat*. The verse means that the place is beautiful and well-constructed, like a beautiful tattoo placed on the back of a hand.

had buried there. He thought about the way the Turkish friend pronounced most of the Arabic letters with an accent, and how he mocked the Arab Spring and believed that it was a failure. None of them wanted to admit, including the history teacher, that he was making fun of them. They allowed him because they believed he held the key to their fortune. Thus, they ignored many of his trespasses.

His memory sank in the dampness of the cold night, and his pains multiplied like worms over a tender corpse. A dull tear ran out of the corner of his eye like a slow turtle.

They arrived in Amman and got into a service car that took them to the Interior Ministry Circle, where they were going to split, for eternity.

Ahmad and his brother got out at the roundabout that was full of people and lost in the bustle of the noise. The two young men walked, unguided, to where they did not know.

The large security presence in the city made Ahmad nervous and suspicious. Meanwhile, Khalid pulled his head high in pride every time he passed by a Darak. He saw himself in them and constantly tried to get close to them. He wanted to know about their lives, how they spent their days, and their work, which seemed exciting and important to a young man who rarely left his village and knew nothing about life except its small dreams.

The sky seemed closer, the buildings that boldly reached up to the clouds, countless cars, and so many people—more than the earth could hold. The honking of the car horns was deafening, and their fumes suffocating.

Ahmad stopped beside one of the people and dared asking him about the reason for the protest that was taking place.

The man shook his head, wrinkled his mouth, and kept walking. He walked up to one of the policemen and asked, but the man walked away and left Ahmad with no answers.

He decided to go do what he was asked to do by the sheikh and later come back to discover the secret of what was going on in the roundabout,[†] which was always in the news.

Ahmad said goodbye to his little brother Khalid. They exchanged an embrace, kisses on each cheek, glances, tears, and small sighs about a bitter reality leading them to a steep *"barren valley,"*[‡] with no hope.

Each went his way with their small hands waving goodbye. Khalid was lost in the bustle of the crowd, and Ahmad went on to deliver the envelope for the sheikh who warned him that he would not have mercy on him if he did not deliver his charge and do his job.

Khalid boarded the military bus that moved slowly through the crowded streets where people crossed the roads as if something was burning in their chests or as if they were running away from a wild beast, jumping into the unknown. The bus shrouded with fear crossed other groups that were duller and less fearful and moved slowly passing the chanters. The noise of the bus was louder than the chants of the crowd. It intertwined with voices making it hard for Khalid to hear the chants clearly. The bus was taking him on a road, and he did not know where it would end.

"For me Allah sufficeth, and He is the best disposer of affairs."[§] Khalid heard this through the black wool crochet hat that his sister had made for him, and wondered what that tall man with a dry, shaved face was concerned about.

The lump on the man's cheeks gave the impression that he was a criminal and scary, but his invocation brought peace to Khalid's heart.

[†] Al-Dakhliyah Roundabout is located in a square in the heart of the Jordanian capital, Amman, specifically in the Abdali area. It has historically been a common site for protests and an organizing point for demonstrations.

[‡] In reference to the "barren valley" mentioned in surah Ibrahim, verse 37, where Abraham settled some of his offspring in hope of God's favor, asking God to make the hearts of people inclined toward them and provide them with fruits.

[§] A common invocation that indicates disappointment and reliance on God, mainly when someone feels that they are treated unjustly or are facing a crisis.

Khalid surprised the man by asking him, "Who are you asking Allah for protection from?"

The man looked at Khalid who appeared to him like a small bird that had not eaten for a week, sinking in the corner of the chair, his wool hat covering his head and making him look even smaller.

Khalid looked away, then looked at the man, who said, "The bad illegitimate people left nothing for the good, legitimate ones."

Khalid turned his face away and looked out the window at the crowd and said, "I don't understand, sir?"

The man cleared his throat and said what made Khalid uncomfortable. "Why do the Darak confront these unarmed men? Isn't there a more civilized way to communicate with them?"

Khalid was confused and could not figure out how people thought anymore. This seemed mixed up to him. His small eyes retreated again, and went on following what was happening, and watching the Darak standing like a shield in front of some in a huge crowd.

He then heard a faint voice of another man, as if he were responding to the first man, say, "Allah bless and protect the brave men of the Darak. By Allah, if it were not for them, the country would have been devoured by gangs and terrorists. May Allah protect them, protect our country, and maintain the bounty of peace and security."

The response galvanized Khalid's spirit who was huddling, hurt, and confused in the corner of his chair. He felt like clapping. He wanted to laugh loudly, to jump joyfully out of the window into the lines of the Darak that walked in long serried lines on the sides of the street. He was flooded with joy.

Nothing broke his happiness except for the sound of the bell pressed by the tall man sitting near him.

Khalid's eyes followed the tall man getting out of the bus and walking away. He wished he could know why he was angry with the Darak and the reason for his dismay with the show of force, the signs of security and peace, but he did not know.

He took a small piece of paper out of his pocket, looked at it, and could not tell clearly what was written on it. He had finished ninth grade without learning to write one meaningful sentence, and had difficulty reading too. This did not bother him. He was still happy by the answer the tall man who vanished in the mass of the crowds in the street received.

Khalid showed the paper to the boy sitting next to him, who was younger, asking for his help with figuring out the street address. The boy suggested that he get off at the next stop and walk to his destination.

Khalid looked at the younger boy who could read and felt like blaming himself for not learning what he needed to learn at school, but instead he hid his sadness, smiled, and addressed the boy in what sounded somewhat sarcastic, "We the children of the villages, learn to read late, after we experience life, and explore the city too."

Khalid looked again at the face of the young boy who was clean, wearing a neat outfit, carrying a notebook decorated with colors, and added, "I mean Amman, in particular."

The young boy smiled and asked, "Do you mean to say that we in the city learn how to read, then learn Amman after that?"

"Yes"

"Even we are becoming strangers in Amman now. Amman is not ours, like it is not yours."

The man with his head wrapped in a red keffiyeh lost his patience.⁵ His ears almost pierced his headcover listening to the conversation between the boys in the seat behind him. He turned his face and looked at them impatiently and said, "Don't you see that we are not fair to Amman when we call it a city, especially we who come to it from the surrounding areas and are still bound to life in the villages which guards our consciousness. We bring it with us. Boys, Amman is still a large

---

⁵ The red and white keffiyeh is usually worn by Jordanian men, especially in winter. Increasingly, it is becoming a symbol of identity and cultural pride, celebrated in songs and pop-culture.

village. The city in not measured by its buildings but by the awareness of the people who live in it."

This talk was too big for Khalid. He nudged the boy sitting next to him, asking him to ring the bell for the bus to stop. He creased his lips and raised his eyebrows in surprise, said goodbye to the boy that sat next to him and the man that entered their conversation without permission, exited the bus, and walked to the street.

Envelope

Ahmad completed his mission and delivered the envelope to its destination. He returned after a few hours to find the circle teeming with people, and full of chants, slogans, and banners. He remembered the events at Ja'far Mosque in his small village and compared the two.

He then approached one of the excited youths with short, loose pants, stopped him, and asked him about the roaring crowd. "Who brought all these people together?"

The boy turned around, looked at the crowd perplexed, placed his hand on his hair, which was shaped like a dry tree, and said, "Love of country, and hatred of the corrupt."

The slogans flew out of the people's mouths like butter on water boiling over an old, wood fire. Ahmad tried inconspicuously to read what was written on the banners and thought that they needed crowds like this at Ja'far Mosque for their voices to be heard. They needed something that would bring out the crowd.

Ahmad suddenly remembered his promise to the sheikh to be back in the village the next day after completing his assignment.

He left the crowd and walked toward the line of taxis for shared rides under the Ministry of Interior bridge where the crowd gathered and the cries rose high.

Ahmad did not realize that there were three different groups exchanging words and chants in the roundabout. Shortly after arriving, the scene became heated and volatile. The crowds were made to cram together.

Ahmad walked to an old man sitting on a wooden bench waiting for a taxi that was late because of the protest blocking the road and asked, "Who are these people?"

The old man laughed loudly, mentioned something that Ahmad did not know the meaning of—"the loyalists"—then turned his face away and looked at the street drowning with people and cars, and added, "These are the ones that prevent the taxis from getting to us. They are the ones that are making us late. They are blocking the street and stopping traffic."

Two groups faced each other while the security forces watched. The place was littered with stones, sticks, and empty bottles. The security forces fully understood what was going on. They backed off a little, allowing the taxis to come through. The old man got into the car and Ahmad followed, sat next to him, and they left the scene; Ahmad had a great desire to stay, but he did not.

The old man poked his head out of the partially opened window that the driver had locked to prevent the passengers from messing with it. He took a deep breath, then turned his face to Ahmad.

The old man then took a cloth handkerchief out of his pocket, spit in it, cleared his throat to get the attention of the rest of the passengers, and said, "Loyalists and opposition. Ah, I wish it were for the country."

He spat in the handkerchief again, put it back in his pocket, and went back to looking out the window with his sunken eyes.

Images and ideas crowded Ahmad's mind, and he recalled his childhood memories of the image of his brother. Although he was on his way to become a member of the Darak, which had the greatest presence in the streets and the alleys, he felt afraid when the car passed by one of them in uniform and full gear. He recalled what he saw in the circle and remembered how they took the side of the loyalists against the opposition and beat the protestors. This made him angry, and he thought of himself as a candle that shines more brightly when darkness spreads around it.

The old man turned his face, which looked in the dark like the face of a fox, toward Ahmad when the car entered the tunnel at the third roundabout in the middle of the capital; his were eyes full of talk, drowned in pain and fear, and he said, "In 1956, when we served in the National Guard, I was a boy your age. The opposition parties came out against the Baghdad Accord. They brought us to the streets to beat up the opposition, but we did not have the heart to do so."

His wounded memory was dripping pain, which he fought to stop and continued, "The opposition was a true opposition, and the soldiers were true soldiers, and the regime was a true regime. Everyone worried and cared for the country."

The old man sighed, buried his nose in his cloth handkerchief, and added, "Today, everything is backward. They distort nationalism, and honor mediocracies."

When they arrived at the transportation center, Ahmad said goodbye to the old man. He then took the bus back to Karak, leaving behind Amman, drowning in a pile of black smoke.

The bus followed the road through a sea of barren desert, while the passengers held their breath, avoiding its sand that was more damaging and harmful when it wrapped them in its grip unexpectedly.

A car moving in the opposite direction carried Yusuf and Abu Khalil to Amman.

Yusuf's constant sighs and complaints made clear his distain, disgust, and disloyalty for the country where he was born. During this long desert trip, listening to Muhammad Abdu's song, "The Places," Abu Khalil reflected on what the history teacher did and said and realized for the first time how he saw the country. Abu Khalil believed that all the patriotism the history teacher talked about was falsehoods and deception. It was a guard set up to protect the vicious foxes who sank their teeth into the flesh of what we metaphorically call "the homeland."

Abu Khalil who spent a large part of his life in service to the country began to sway little by little away from his pride and patriotism under the badgering of the history teacher with his vast knowledge, eloquent speech, and ability to persuade. Abu Khalil felt like a small bird with a flood of bullets targeted at him, hitting his head but not killing him.

The old man realized that he was losing the battles. Although the history teacher continued his attack, he started enjoying what he was saying, assumptions and ideas that revealed to the old man the fallacy of his life and his grave defeat. He imagined himself, now, standing under the sun, wanting to be washed of his sins. His memory flared, like a tree of snakes, shaken by the strong wind, eager to tear his legacy. He forced himself to forget, but the man was loaded with guilt and the history teacher continued to pour salt on his open wounds.

Abu Khalil gazed at Amman as they approached the city. "Amman is not Amman anymore."

Yusuf interrupted him, "A sinful city that has exposed her thighs stained with the semen of others, and become a prostitute desired by all Arabs."

"Although I do not know if you meant to praise or offend, I mean something else. I meant to say that she has matured, grown, and become more beautiful than other cities."

"Man, you babble about what you don't know."

Yusuf said that and turned his face away while Abu Khalil was still looking at his scarred face and thinking, "Are cities like women?

"Is there a city that prostitutes herself?

"Who are her customers?

Then he thought to himself, "This man is going too far—he has to be stopped."

Every time Abu Khalil wanted to respond harshly to the stupid mass of fat that he was dealing with, the words stuck in his throat, worrying about his interests, and fearful that the teacher would leave him in Amman alone, without achieving his ambitions and getting what he came to Amman for.

The teacher's words continued to resonate horribly inside him. He could hear the cries of the poor city with its bustling life, tormented by the fact that he was no longer her faithful soldier.

The crowded city swallowed the fancy car of the history teacher, which he had recently purchased after the pitcher deal, and swallowed Abu Khalil who gazed through the car window at the faces of the passersby. He started seeing through the lanterns of his memories, through the darkness that was brought on by his companion—a prophet without a prophecy.

"Don't talk too much. The people that we are going to meet do not like too much talk, and you blabber a lot."

Abu Khalil swallowed the teacher's offensive words that made him fearful and suspicious, but said nothing. He was worried that he would be unable to soar in this city without the contacts of the history teacher, whose promises had not come through yet.

The car stopped at a street corner in the city. Their contact entered a liquor store, bought a couple of bottles, placed them on the table in front of them, started drinking, and put forward his offer to Abu Khalil.

They would not deal with the man who had a thoub and an embroidered abaya* in the back seat of his car. The fancy car then stopped in front of a large building. Yusuf and Abu Khalil walked into a big office. They were met and welcomed by a tall, dark man who whispered something to Yusuf about the pitcher and other upcoming deals. They talked about a more profitable deal, opening new possibilities.

Abu Khalil was listening but could not say anything. Soon, the history teacher told him about what just happened.

---

* Traditional man's robe and embroidered outer cover. It implies that the customer is a wealthy man from the Gulf, Qatar, or Saudi Arabia.

On the way back, the history teacher let Abu Khalil in on his secret. He dreamed about becoming the Minister of Tourism and Antiquities.

He dreamed about his bags going through customs without being searched, so that he could take with him whatever he wanted. "These people are powerful. They are the ones that want to nominate me for this position."

He threw around a few more vague statements; Abu Khalil was unable to keep up with what he was saying. All that he was dreaming about was owning a fancy car, becoming a respectable leader, and be given priority in everything.

He turned his face to the history teacher and asked, "What would I get out of this?"

"You will be my right hand.

"The one who will put my plans into action, away from the spotlight."

The car of the history teacher, with his deferred prophecies, took them back to the road to the south, faraway and forgotten.

Picture

Khalid arrived, tired, at a large gate with a huge picture of the King wearing the Darak uniform. A sense of pride and vanity filled the boy looking at the master of the land wearing his uniform. He raised his head high and stared at the picture. He saw the outlines of his future that were absent from his sad childhood, the dark village, the boring school, and the graveyards that oozed pain and agony. He wanted to be rid of his fear. His dreams widened when he looked at the picture, larger than life.

He told himself, "This is me, Abu Khalil. I will be back. And I will know how to get back at you and the history teacher."

He drew subtle strength from the picture. It appeared at times smiling and at other times staring back from the distance. Sometimes, he saw it as the father he was waiting for, bringing back his childhood that escaped at the threshold of the graveyards.

His imagination broke down recent events and reconstructed them, distorting them at times, and focusing them at others; the wounds in his heart were still bleeding. His young mind embraced the picture, constantly checking it out; the full face in the picture pleased him and its figure and posture looked strong and manly.

His dry lips dared to utter a muffled word that summed up his dreams, "Ah! If he was my father. . ."

His reflection asked, "What do you mean?"

"I mean, a son of a King. I mean, Abu Khalil and the lowlife Yusuf, mere cockroaches that I could squash with my feet and keep walking."

His reflection laughed a despicable laugh that echoed in the chambers of his heart and said, "Don't kid yourself. Abu Khalil and Yusuf are not small. They are too big for you to think that you can get rid of them."

Khalid walked forward and placed a small bag that he was carrying on his shoulder.

While he was daydreaming, several armored vehicles crossed the road near him. They were carrying men in helmets and wearing bulletproof vests as if they were going to a battle. The King in the picture was still there raising his hand, waving. The boys were never sure if he was waving goodbye to the men on their way to carrying out their missions or welcoming those arriving with bags that carried their dreams, who had nowhere else to place them.

He looked admirably at the men in the vehicles behind the machine guns. His eyes followed them as they disappeared on the distant roads.

He reached the center's gate and was allowed to enter after the guard made sure that he was one of the new recruits.

They welcomed him and took him to a spacious room that he shared with several other men. He settled in the majestic castle.*

He did not sleep well that night despite his excitement and love for his new dream. He was tossing in a bed that he was not used to after

---

* Referring to Karak Castle, one of the oldest and largest castles in the Levant. It dates to the antiquity period and was settled by the Nabataeans. It was later part of Roman Arabia, and then it was fortified and used as a military garrison during the Crusades. It was later conquered by the Mamluks who expanded the castle, and then by the Ottomans who destroyed part of it.

filling his stomach with food that he had never eaten before. He rubbed his head, which resembled a potato after the military barber shaved it, without paying attention to the scars on his head that had started to hurt.

He stood up and examined his new blue uniform, American-made boots, and holster.

He looked at his boots again and remembered his father screaming in the face of his cousin, Khalil, who was selling new, stolen military boots and green-khaki camouflage uniforms that he used to steal from his friends, saying "Allah is Great, Khalil. I am your uncle, man. The boots for ten dinars? Allah is Great. Such an injustice! By Allah, I will be willing to go back and serve in the army before buying it from you. What would you have asked for if it wasn't stolen?"

His eyes filled with tears when he remembered his father. "How I wish I had been here before you died. I wish you could hear me now. I would've bought you all the army's boots you wanted."

He crawled under his blue damp blanket on the bed that squeaked every time he moved.

The image of Khalil, his cousin, the son of Abu Khalil that broke the heart of his father swung in front of him through the darkness of the chamber filled with the snores of the recruits.

He fell asleep, tired, haunted by the images of his people.

Prayer Beads

Um Ahmad was counting the days on the pendulum of her prayer beads, with a thousand beads passing the time through her fingertips, tossing the moments in a swirl of waiting, like a piece of foam floating over the pain surrounding the small island that she had created for herself.

She heard a knock at the gate, and in a fleeting moment, like a deer running away from a leopard, she gathered her beads and stood up. Her departed husband was always on her mind, which turned into sponge absorbing pain.

She recalled the details of her life with him and things that they hoped to do but did not.

She remembered how they danced on their wedding night when he told her, "I am now a soldier, but tomorrow I will be an officer. You need to learn to dance like the wives of important people—to dance to their rich husbands' music."

She remembered how he gave her that night a red sleeping gown, which he had bought a while before and hid from her to surprise her with on their first night together. He put it on her so that she would feel beautiful like the women she saw in the movies. She looked at her reflection in the mirror that he placed by the ledge of the window to shave his face, and smiled, left her sorrows behind for a moment, licked her lips to give them some color, and felt the stiff braids under her headcover.

The knock on the gate stopped, and Ahmad walked in like a painting in the cloud of black smoke she was drowning in. Her heart sank, her limbs drooped, her eyes shut, her head hit something, and she recalled hymns of misery that had befallen them.

Ahmad greatly missed her. He kissed her hand and walk with her into the house. Her husband's image itched painfully in her memory subsided, and her focus turned to her son. She asked about the reason for his long absence, about his brother that went with him to Amman, and about his trip.

Ahmad was guarded in his answers, and she was asking, eagerly wanting to know.

He took some money out of his pocket and placed it in her trembling hand while looking away.

"Buy us some food that we might forget the bread and tea days."

Ahmad's words and the large sum of money in her hand worried her. She held the money and asked Ahmad, "What's wrong with bread and tea? Didn't it make a perfect man out of you? Also, where did you get all this money from?"

He came near her, and with a flood of tenderness asked, "Are we destined to be miserable forever? Don't you want us to get out of the situation we are in? Don't you want us to add things to our table that are lacking? Don't you want us to change our world that is lacking food, lacking love, lacking morals, lacking honest politics, and lacking good men? Don't you see that our men are bread and tea, Um Ahmad?

"Don't you see that Abu Khalil, who is in my opinion, even less than bread and tea, is the master of our miserable world? He and Yusuf are willing to sell their honor for an old antique."

Ahmad remembered his past—tenderness mixed with fear—in his mother's fingertips combing through his hair, and the history teacher insisting that he introduce his father to him.

Ahmad pretended to sleep after he laid his head in his mother's lap. He was basking in her loving kindness and realizing what it meant to lose a father, still at the threshold of life and the door of inquiry. A bitterness filled his mouth. He felt that he was a child, naked, being cared for by his mother. He wished that he could break the wall of silence that separated them and return to her womb, safe and protected.

He realized how stupid the world was, when he slightly opened his eyes and saw his mother's tears, and her hand patting his head, lulling him. She was waiting for the answer from a son that she had raised, and with him growing up, her questions grew, waiting for answers.

Her words came muffled like a slaughtered sheep, "You didn't tell me about your brother? Where did you leave him? Where is he now?"

He answered her and fell back to sleep. His words seemed to her like dripping honey in a bitter and dark night. "He is in a better place than where you and I are. At least he is eating at a table better than ours. He is not eating only bread and tea. He is not living in misery like you and I are."

The next day, Ahmad met the sheikh at Ja'far Mosque. The sheikh expressed his admiration for Ahmad. He honored him and rewarded him more than generously. This puzzled Ahmad—a million questions ran through his head. "What does the sheikh expect from me in return?"

"Why me?"

The questions disturbed Ahmad's loneliness and worried him.

Despite the ambiguity that surrounded the sheikh, Ahmad decided to take advantage of his influence, contacts, and skills. He hoped that the sheikh would be an asset for him in his determination to seek revenge on his uncle.

The sheikh talked to Ahmad about jihad,* the war in Syria, and the importance of supporting the mujahedeen† to raise the words of Allah on earth and beneath every sky. He told him that the mujahedeen are the ones who will rid the world of corruption, straighten the Faith of God, and raise its banner. He told him that at this time, religion has become the profession of those who have no profession, and thus, if it becomes necessary to fight, they will. An intentional tear fell out of the sheikh's eye.

He was watching Ahmad's body language and reactions while repeating contrived words, "God will lead to this Faith men who will support it, and I see you are one of them! Your energy and determination, no doubt, will be put in its rightful place."

The sheikh held Ahmad's wrist, looked into his eyes, slapped him on his leg and said, "You have become a man and a fighter."

The sheikh got up. His words circled inside the mind of the fragile boy. They went quickly from his ears to his heart, and he felt a tremor in his chest, a fear mixed with pleasure.

The sheikh paced the mosque's floor talking about jihad and linked it to corruption that we see and hear about in every corner of government institutions. He mentioned the need to learn lessons about jihad, here in Allah's land, before we gathered for the ultimate battle that we were mobilizing for here in the land of the resurrection.

The sheikh was recalling a historical narrative based on a story stuffed with interpretations, legends, and dreams that accompanied hundreds of generations about a postponed victory, soon approaching. However, Ahmad's awaited battle was with his uncle, Abu Khalil. His uncle's image did not leave his mind—whenever he spoke about jihad, he imagined him as his enemy. Whenever he talked about corruption, he imagined him as the most corrupt, and whenever the sheikh talked

---

* It is an Arabic word that literally means "striving" or "struggling." In Islamic context, it refers to any effort to make personal and social life conform to God's guidance. In Islamic law, it refers to armed struggle against unbelievers, while modernist Islamic scholars generally equate it with defensive warfare.

† The Arabic term for people engaged in jihad.

about the "permissible" and "forbidden" according to Allah, Ahmad was convinced that the one who suspended that law was his uncle.

The sheikh walked to the gate of the empty mosque, speaking forcefully as if he was talking a crowd. "There are major thieves that steal everything, and enjoy everything, while you and your brother don't even have bread and tea. As soon as a glimpse of hope opens for your father, may Allah have mercy upon his soul, he is confronted by those who pretend to love this country but manipulate the standard of "permissible' and "forbidden" when they know nothing about it."

The words of the sheikh resonated in the boy's heart, formed his understanding, and suspended his thinking. He was tossed into a raging passion which toyed with his mind and scattered it like small pieces of paper in a seething storm.

The image of his mother, sister, brother, and father laid to rest in the city of the dead, hundreds of meters away, occupied his mind.

Thinking of his uncle provoked him, creating an urgency to do something. He stood up and said, "I want to train for jihad in Syria."

The sheikh's heart danced with joy. Confident, he instructed his victim on how to be balanced and calm when making decisions. "Be patient my son. You will get your share, sooner or later."

Ahmad kneeled, his breathing became heavy, and he pleaded to go. "Please help me. I want to go to jihad." He wanted nothing more from life than to come back, strong and wealthy, so that he could fight his uncle and punish him.

The sheikh finally agreed, and Ahmad's heart danced with joy. And suddenly, Ahmad felt a fear of the unknown and thought about what would happen to his mother and sister.

The sheikh stood up and walked in a slow pace. Ahmad followed him, showing reverence. The sheikh turned, looked at him, and placed his hand over his head.

His eyes glowed, confident that he had Ahmad where he wanted him and said, "I hope we meet here again. We will be testing you in the next few days on a big mission, a type of jihad. Be ready. May Allah bless you."

He pulled his hand away while setting his gaze into Ahmad's eyes, then left him and walked out in a hurry. He abruptly stopped and turned to Ahmad, who was walking behind him.

"Say goodbye to your mother because you don't know when you'll be coming back. You might be gone for a long time."

The sheikh continued walking, then turned back again and said, "You will come back a man. You know what I mean. We will know what to do if you come back. You are one of our loyal soldiers."

Like arrows, the sheikh's words went through Ahmad's head. His mind could no longer process the ambiguity of the sheikh's words. Nevertheless, the sheikh became the guide in the absence of the dead father, the history teacher chasing after antiques and profit, Abu Khalil, unaware, consumed with playing with the big boys, and Jamal moving abroad tired of nepotism and corruption.

Early in the morning, Ahmad said goodbye to his mother and got into the sheikh's car, which seemed fancier than the cars of Abu Khalil's guests. They drove east, through the darkness of the desert, followed by Um Ahmad's eyes watching them disappear behind the eastern hills.

Abu Khalil was awake and recognized the sheikh that took his nephew in his fancy car. His suspicions were ignited, and many questions crossed his mind.

He wondered, "Who is this fat sheikh?

"Is he an undercover intelligence agent?

"Perhaps he is a customer looking for antiques?

"Perhaps the boy is digging with someone else and found a precious piece?

"I'll send you to where I sent his father if that is true."

Abu Khalil watched the sheikh's car until it left the village.

The sheikh emphasized to Ahmad the importance of appearance, which was needed to be accepted by the group. His hissing voice mixed with the sound of the recitation of the Quran, coming from the tape in the car, fell on Ahmad's ear like the beating of a pendulum on a scary and dark night.

"Your appearance commands power and authority and makes you distinguished. Thus, you must let your beard grow, and pull your thoub up, and shave your mustache. Although your beard is not fully defined yet, it will grow stronger with shaving, just like your faith that is growing by the day."

The sheikh said this looking into Ahmad's eyes, touching his soft facial hair, while watching for the potholes in the road, and added, "These hairs aren't void of faith, and your tender bones will be solid. Your small chest holds a strong heart pulsing with faith!"

The car carrying Ahmad and the sheikh arrived after a long drive at Zarqa. The city seemed full of fear and bewilderment. The sheikh stopped and picked up some sweets, got back into his car, and drove through the narrow alleys of the city. As he drove, he pointed out the police and security cars, stirring up Khalid against them while devouring the sweets he bought with a great appetite.

The sheikh stopped his car in an empty alley, got out, and told Ahmad to do so. Ahmad followed him, walking through alleys on the west side of town. They climbed the few steps of a building, then the sheikh stopped and looked to his right and left. He waited a little to make sure he was not followed, came down the stairs, and rang a bell.

An old sheikh opened the door. They shook hands, and the sheikh that brought him kissed the old one's hand, whispered something in his ear, patted Ahmad's back, and left without saying a word.

Ahmad was shaking. His chest too small for his violently pounding heart. This filthy place was not big enough for him. He felt that the world was lining up against him and not giving him a chance in life. He walked with his new master into a lightless, underground room. The silence was interrupted by the footsteps on the street above, mixed with the breathing of the old sheikh like the sound of a train going through a distant desert.

Ahmad spent his miserable days, living in this hellhole, chasing a dream. Meanwhile, the old sheikh watched Ahmad and followed the progress of his growing beard.

The street and the sidewalk by the edge of his room were full of beautiful women, which Ahmad could see only through a small opening at the level of the sidewalk. The heels of their shoes pounding the street excited him. He watched part of their bodies passing by and tried to get glimpses that would feed his sexual imagination. He entered the bathroom with its intense stench three to four times a day, just to masturbate. It consumed him and ruined his nerves and senses. His mind was disrupted by his sexual frustration growing stronger through his isolation. It went from dreaming about a woman smiling at him in his village, to thinking that his manliness was insulted if he saw the heel of a passing woman and did not get aroused.

A month passed while Ahmad lived in this small prison with nothing but the old sheikh, yellow books, and a small opening that provided him with air, light, and dreams of love and freedom. He had plenty of time to think about jihad, victory, and eventually defeating his uncle, the false prophet (his history teacher), and being sent to Paradise and receiving his share of beautiful huris.‡

The old sheikh did nothing but pray, recite the Quran, and read yellow books that filled the place with their odor. This was supposed to be a time for Ahmad's learning and reflection in preparation to become ready for jihad. Other than growing his beard, and having plenty of time on his hands, Ahmad received little guidance. He sat on an old, tattered couch, forcing himself to pray with the sheikh, sometimes out of courtesy, and without ablutions at other times.

The old sheikh approached him one night and aroused his suspicions when he asked, "Do you really want to become a mujahid?"

He then smiled a faded smile and continued with a sharp and painful question. "Or is there someone who pushed you into this basement, and from here, to another permanent one that you don't know when or how you will be sent to?"

Ahmad tried to ignore the last question and its implications, but he could not. Some words are like penetrating arrows, if fired, they do not go back. The statement fell hard into his heart, and he had a hard time

---

‡ The plural of *huri* or *huriah*, a beautiful virgin maiden who awaits devout Muslims in Paradise or Heaven.

processing it. It continued to pound inside him every time he heard the old sheikh's scratchy voice or his call to prayer.

The coldness of the nights intensified, and the stars, which he counted and dreamed of reaching one night, disappeared. The desolate place became more desolate and terrifying when it became cold, and the lights of the streets and houses were cut off by an untimely winter storm. Meanwhile, at a far corner of his house, a small candle was fighting the breeze, coming through an opening at the upper side of the wall, which the old sheikh attempted to close with a green military cover.

There were knocks on the door, three consecutive knocks, then two, followed by one. The old sheikh looked at Ahmad and said, "Open, it's your teacher."

Ahmad did not fully understand what the old sheikh meant, and quickly asked, "Who is he?"

The old sheikh scolded him sharply, "Open the door when I tell you and don't ask."

The harsh answer of the man who had stayed quiet and hardly said much during the past months bothered Ahmad, but he soon forgot about it when the old sheikh got up, hugged him, and asked him to gather his things.

It had not crossed Ahmad's mind that he would be leaving to anywhere. He could not think of anyone at that point except his mother. He wished he could go to her, kiss her head and hands. He wished that he could get out of this basement and return to his simple life and dreams.

The old sheikh stood quickly, like an arrow, muttering, "Quickly, the car is coming.

"Learn these roads well.

"You might need to come back.

"It is time to say goodbye."

The old sheikh carried some of Ahmad's belongings and went out. They stood by the door.

The driver of the new Jeep waited for Ahmad to get in. The old sheikh came closer and gave him a gentle and tender hug. Ahmad was touched—he never had that type of tender intimacy with his father, who was loving in his own way, but not physically affectionate. Abu Ahmad was hard to talk to at times and did not hesitate to slap him at any moment, but he knew that he loved him.

Then, the old sheikh watched them leave.

Ahmad watched him through the rear window of the vehicle as they drove away.

Then the old sheikh disappeared underground again, and the Jeep went on its way, out of the city, drowned in the darkness.

Amid the darkness, Ahmad envisioned images of a coming battle with swords and recalled the sight of the old sheikh disappearing underground, in the darkness, in a city full of bright lights.

Foggy images reminded Ahmad that he was in a desert, full of fear, alienation, and cruelty.

He could not help himself. He wanted to cry, but he was embarrassed to do so.

He wondered fearfully, "Are they really taking me to jihad?"

Revenge

Khalid's heart calmed down from the flood of fear that had consumed it in the past. He was looking forward to growing amid the culture of orders and duties that he faced in his new world. The strict regimen of the camp needed patience and endurance. It forced him to grow, physically and emotionally, under the watchful eyes of his trainer.

The features of the tanned trainer resembled, to a large degree, his father's. He remembered when his father ploughed the land for the farmers for a fee, using the red horse he had. It was a wild animal that no one could touch and became an obedient creature, faithfully pulling the plough. He recalled how his father used pieces of cardboard to create blinders that he fixed on the head of the horse to limit its vision. This way the horse could only see what was in front of it and did not get distracted with anything that happened to its sides. That image was still fresh in Khalid's mind.

His father's horse did not deviate from its path and did not fail to plow, nor did it hesitate to go where his father wanted it to go. His father was satisfied with the way the horse turned out, but he became sad when he saw the horses in the village come out to race, competing for titles, while his horse became dull and tired, and was unable to keep up with the other horses. His horse did not even bother shaking its head asking for its feed, or neigh like the other horses did.

"What made me think about my father's horse?" He thought about that when he saw several horses get ready for a mission outside the walls of the castle that he had been living in for the last six months.

Khalid was convinced that his strong trainer was dealing with him like his father treated his horse. His father placed blinders on the horse, and his trainer was placing a heavy helmet on Khalid's head. His father was more merciful to his horse's head than this trainer was to his.

Khalid, who was barely eighteen years old, realized that he was in the circle of attention, and that his body was being prepared for a difficult mission—not the one he dreamed of and desired, to face Abu Khalil and the history teacher in their village. He started to realize this after a conversation with one of the recruits from the third barracks, who was from the Ja'far region like him, where most of the youth, like many others from the south, joined the Darak—even the ones that finished high school—because they believed that it was their best path to prosperity in the absence of a good government job, and because of the lack of development and reform in the south where they lived.

His friend whispered to him that they would be facing the crowds that riot each Friday, and that he would be asked to keep the peace. He further explained that Khalid's battle would not be with Abu Khalil and the history teacher and the people that they represented, but with the riotous crowd that intended to harm the country.

Bread and tea and Abu Khalil and Yusuf were no longer the focus of the battle. Khalid's horizon widened and new thoughts emerged, tightening their grip on his mind, constantly there, like the helmet of a soldier who had just come out of a grueling battle, hanging onto a branch of a small tree.

Khalid rebelled against this awareness when he secretly fought his fears, and asked his dauntless trainer about the nature of the mission that they were preparing for.

The question hit the trainer like a lightning bolt.

He turned to Khalid who was physically fit but scared when the trainer yelled at him. "Where is your gun holstered?

"Where is your helmet?"

Fear returned to Khalid's young heart. He touched his head and felt the helmet on it, reached his hand to his waist, and felt the gun secure in its holster.

He backed off a little and tried to understand why his trainer asked him about his helmet and his gun. He looked a little further and remembered his father's horse that he made compliant.

Khalid walked alone, sad, thinking about the world behind these walls, conjuring up his mother with her white hair scattered on one side of her face while she dried her tears upon his departure.

Khalid began preparing to face the enemy behind the walls. He embarked on learning new skills that suggested to him that all the world that lived beyond the walls of this fortress looked like his uncle, Abu Khalil, and the history teacher. These images were classified in his mind as enemies and criminals.

The obsession for revenge grew considerably and expanded in his mind, and it began to narrow. He developed a desire to satisfy his lust to fight, especially now when his shoulders broadened, and his muscles grew strong as he faithfully completed all the training.

He imagined the monsters that killed his father's dreams and forced him to leave his mother, his young sister, and his brother who was missing.

The troops were distributed to the various units in the field. Finally, his assignment came; he was sent to a camp in the north.

He wanted to go to the south to be close to his mother. He still believed that she was not safe from his uncle. He also wanted to be close to his uncle to be able to control him, but he followed the orders of his commanders and joined the North Battalion.

The night when he left his training camp for the north camp, he was as proud as if he were going to conquer the cities of the north and annex them into his kingdom.

At that same night, Ahmad found himself lost in a sea of bullets. When the darkness cleared, he saw a group of men riding in four-wheel-drive vehicles with machine guns surrounded by crowds that resembled a battlefield, with troops trying to regroup.

Transformation

Ahmad and the sheikh, who brought him from Zarqa, got out of the car. The sheikh took the leader aside and whispered something in his ear.

Ahmad did not dare to ask where he was, and he could not say anything so as not to appear stupid, or look scared, cowardly, or hesitant.

It was important for him to reflect the image of a submissive mujahid looking to uphold the word of Allah. A boy about his age approached and welcomed him.

"Welcome Sheikh Abu We'am al-Karaki."

He said that with a sad glance in his eyes, surrounded by dark circles of fear and suspicion, sowing big questions in Ahmad's heart. As if he was saying to Ahmad, "Why did you come here?

"Who seduced you?

"Did they seduce you like they seduced me?

"My condolences to your mother who is waiting to mourn you?"

Ahmad looked at the innocent round face of the boy and saw through the dim light a few hairs scattered over his face under the pretext of faith, sprouting aimlessly.

A strange feeling crept into his chest. Was it fear?

Or was it pride that he did not want to show?

Or was it the ring of the strange and big name he was given, killing his childhood and dreams, and turning him into another person?

Ahmad was surprised that the boy knew the nickname he had received in that isolated house in Zarqa by the old sheikh, a city that was more barren than the desert.

Ahmad approached the boy and asked, "How did you know my name?"

The boy answered confidently, "You are now one of us, all you have to do is follow orders."

Ahmad felt like a fish out of water, a fish that had just left a roaring ocean where it roamed freely and played as it pleased, to the bottom of a suffocating trap, jumping into the air, looking for an escape, only to fall back into the muck of the fisherman's net.

He tried to convince himself that he was not a commodity, or a number, but he failed.

He thought about his friend, the fat sheikh who recruited him, who brought him from under the wing of darkness filled with fear, and who left him in Zarqa without a proper goodbye—without looking into his eyes, seeing him, in the darkness that he had drowned him in.

Did he think that, if he had looked into his eyes, the heart of the executioner would have softened and he would have pardoned his victim?

A short man with thick hair, a long beard, a voice that sounded like hissing, and small teeth, looked at Ahmad and ordered him to ride in the back of the truck.

The truck drove through the long night. Ahmad fell asleep on a box laying on the bed of the vehicle despite the potholes that made the truck frequently jump into the air. He woke up to the deafening sound of bullets and machine guns shaking the heart of earth and warning the listeners of the approaching terror.

Ahmad's heart felt like it would almost pound itself out of his chest with every passing bullet. He jumped out of the back of the truck; at the same moment the short man who brought him there came out of the vehicle, approached him, and asked, "Do you like jihad, boy?"

The question brought Ahmad, despite his youth, into the thick of the fight, in direct contact with his God, "Yes."

The man smiled, then asked him, still smiling from under his long beard, suggesting a graver scene, and asked, "And women, huris, your reward in heaven?"

Ahmad's heart dropped, but he pulled himself together. He wanted to look strong, and said, "No."

His short answers were drowning in a desert of fear as the short man with the questions left.

Ahmad found himself in a historical Syrian city on the other side of the border. The place was filled with soldiers that seemed as if they were coming out of the Middle Ages. They were tearing at the gates of the ancient city looking for its treasures and defiling its beautiful face.

A minibus filled with veiled girls,* looking for a new life, their eyes dancing under the black fabric covering their faces stopped nearby. Ahmad knew that, as a fighter, he had access to them. His heart quivered with desire, thinking of a night of sex and pleasure. A lock of hair of one of the girls appeared accidently from under her veil. It reminded him of his little sister, turned him off, and spoiled his chance for a passionate night.

A beautiful stone façade covered the building. It was topped with images and statues dating back to a brighter ancient period in the history of the city. He walked closer, looked at it admirably, and remembered Abu Khalil and his father.

What would they do if they were here?

They would have been able to dig up enough glass to sustain them throughout their lives.

Ahmad was pulled out of his daydreams by the whispers of some of the men that sought his help in doing something, but he did not understand

---

*   Refers to *jihad nikah*, sexual jihad, the modern practice by some Muslim women who are sympathetic to Salafi jihadism and travel to warzones, such as Syria, voluntarily offering themselves to be "married" to jihadist militants, often repeatedly and in temporary marriages, providing sexual comfort to help boost the fighters' morale.

what it was. They asked him to carry small, heavy bags. They placed the bags under the beautiful façade, connected them to a detonator, called through loudspeakers "Allah is Great!" and ran away.

Ahmad ran away with them not processing what was going on. They covered their heads with their hands while Ahmad stood there eagerly looking at what was going on. The place exploded and leveled the building, and the call to praise Allah for the success of the mission filled the sky.

What was happening?

How did the scene change?

Who was destroying who?

A tear brought Ahmad back to reality and reignited his yearning for his village and its people.

"Why was I blaming my father? His goal was to provide me with at least bread and tea. This was the extent of his dream. But these people are trying to create a flourishing state amid this ruin."

Ahmad spent months there—a year of suspended death; then he realized, in a fleeting moment, that his death on the soil of his homeland was better. That his jihad, if there is a true jihad, was for his people, and not for the sake of an idea dangling in the sky, heaven, huris, jihad nikah.

He decided to sneak back and return to the city of loneliness and isolation, Zarqa. He was determined to eventually return to Ja'far and its people, to its markets that were still full of mindfulness, resisting change, but not prostituting itself.

Hole

Khalid was watching people from a hole in his heart, through the small opening in the body of the armored vehicle, which was too small for his eyes. He thought about his father and his horse. He was watching the features of the people crowding the streets through the Darak armored vehicle. His heart pounded seeing a woman, while riding in a patrol car one evening, who looked just like his mother. Her image stirred his emotions, and a tear dropped out of his eye bringing with it endless questions. "She looks like my mother . . .

"They are people like us . . .

"Why shouldn't we have mercy on them, as instructed by our trainer?

"Are the people of the north different from the people of the south?

"If it is true what they say, why does this woman look so much like my mother, or perhaps she is my mother who came looking for me?

"Don't these girls look like my sister?

"Isn't this my brother, Ahmad, or someone who looks like him?"

The questions grew on his lips and flooded out of his heart into his mind which was calloused after months of training and reprograming. Like drops of water, the questions fell constantly into a muddy pit, with no noise or echo.

Big questions followed. He drowned them in conversations with his friends about being hungry and wanting to eat, about the kind of food they would be having for dinner, and about their monthly salary and ways to transfer some of it to his mother.

As night settled, bedtime approached with some common orders that were delivered to the soldiers' quarters each night. The heavy questions in his mind started to get to his consciousness and annoy him.

The sound of the soldiers' snores filled the barracks that were big enough for twenty or more beds. The mosquitoes swarmed in the absence of light and bit the sleeping soldiers leaving behind the dirt they gathered through the misery of the days.

Night ended and the golden sun rose into the sky, sneaking through the alleys, the buildings, the windows of the wards, and the distant large barracks where the soldiers lay. The sun fell through the wide windows where the soldiers slept, dragging in its rays, ending the darkness, announcing the start of a new day. The mosquitoes flew away after a final attempt to gather a few drops of blood to sustain themselves, at least for a while, during their short lives.

The sound of the footsteps of the old soldier, who did not sleep, stole the silence of the quiet chambers, which looked at dawn like a strange, pale, and faraway from civilization.

The drill sergeant, who bragged about his youth despite of his long years serving with this regiment, approached. He was aware of the names that they called him in the camp but was not happy to hear them from the new soldiers. He knew that they slept at ten when he ordered lights out, but they still liked to sleep late. He wanted to get revenge on them early in the morning.

He knocked hard on the door of the barracks of the sleeping soldiers and pounded it again with his pace stick. The loud noise startled the soldiers.

They jumped up trembling and disoriented. Khalid woke up thinking that he was drowning in a deep pool of water, fighting death. He stood up, half asleep, stumbling in the room, lost between the beds, looking for his clothes to join his regiment lining up for inspection.

They received important orders that day, which they had not heard the like of before. It was an unusual Friday. The soldiers were getting ready as if they were going to a decisive battle in a long-running war.

The inexperienced soldiers imagined their enemies with massive bodies and hard heads that can only be broken with big, hard truncheons—ghosts coming from beyond, who must be crushed.

Khalid was asking himself as his brain started to slowly wake up, "Is there really an enemy?

"Who is this enemy?

"Is it true what this pot-bellied old soldier, who doesn't even have clear features anymore, says?"

"Who are the enemies?" was the main question that punctured Khalid's mind like a thin needle, entering and exiting his brain with increasing speed, all over.

Fear made Khalid share his question with the drill sergeant. "Who will we be fighting today?"

The drill sergeant, with big black eyes that looked like black circles over a round bronze plate, and shoes like flattened tires, walked to him and yelled, "Ready!"

Khalid had no choice. He got ready following his master's orders, which he delivered from an order he received, canned and ready to consume, like the cans of food delivered to the camp's kitchen.

He then stared in Khalid's face, read something in his eyes and yelled, "Since when do soldiers discuss their orders? Don't you know that we are here to serve the King who keeps this country and its people safe?"

Khalid's heart trembled in his young body that was looking strong and resolute.

Still, he stood up, fixed his eyes on the bronze face, and said boldly, "Yes, we do, sir, but I just wanted to know."

Abu Shafra, as they liked to call the sergeant, grabbed Khalid by his waist and pulled him toward him, testing his strength. He then looked into his eyes and said, "You will see the beards, short thoubs, swords, and daggers today. You will see those who claim to be poor, sidelined, unjustly treated, and other things. You will see and hear a lot today. You will see the crowds come close to your heart, and if you don't defend yourself and your homeland, we will drown in each other's blood."

Khalid lowered his gaze in surrender. Abu Shafra looked at the young soldier's innocent face, and said harshly, "I don't know how you are going to stand up to them when you are so fragile. Don't you know that they are animals?"

"You will see them today with your own eyes."

He let go of Khalid's waist and asked, "Did you have a good breakfast?"

Khalid answered pulling himself together, "Yes, sir. I had good breakfast."

Blood

The sun of that day seemed to pass slowly. It lingered in the sky, unwilling to leave, trying to read and greet people's faces, inspecting their tearful eyes, as if it knew the secret of their lives, fears, and deaths. It wanted to save them with its light, but it was more miserable than death itself. It fell clumsily in its eternal pond, dying to be resurrected again each day. Meanwhile, Ahmad was still contemplating the idea of running away from his group of jihadists. He met up with his Jordanian friend, who like him, was lured to fight with money and the promise of the virgins in heaven. They had a plan.

As they jumped over the barbed wire, on that dreary night, Ahmad recalled his mother's face, which seemed to be holding back anger. After crossing the borders, his main concern was finding a place to shave his beard and change his clothes.

Leaving the jihadists in Syria did not sway Ahmad against jihad. His uncle, Abu Khalil, was getting wealthier after he sold his father's rightful treasure; the history teacher was still practicing his hypocrisy and selling his principles to whomever paid more; and Jamal had given up and left the country to study abroad—his cowardness betrayed his awareness.

His brother, blinded by hunger, was still infatuated with armor-plated vehicles. And his mother, who had lost most of her sight crying over the death of his father and lamenting their hunger and separation, continued counting the days with her prayer beads.

He thought of the fat sheikh, who left him alone in that painful desert night, like a captured, helpless animal, and hundreds like him lured in during a moment of anger, pain, or need.

He recalled his mother's face, poor—except for love—how she used to cut the piece of bread into two equal halves for him and his brother, pour the tea, careful that each of the two cups held equal amounts. He could see the pain of his small village, the relics of its ancient cemetery stolen and sold in broad daylight, with little men taking advantage of it.

"I shaved the hair off my face but did not change my heart," he whispered to his friend under the dim light of the small lantern.

Ahmad and his friend settled in a different city, with people like the people of Ja'far, whom he loved. Overtime, he grew close to the people and settled into the city's paths, small neighborhoods, and narrow alleys. People knew each other and knew their city well. He started his morning walking around, getting into and out of the narrow alleys and wide streets, until the sun settled into the peak of the sky.

At noon, the streets seemed as if they were running with no return, walking in a hurry in four directions, as if the city were in a race with itself without knowing. The city's buildings rippled in the dull atmosphere, its windows like cat's eyes glowing on a cold night.

A man wearing a military coat without buttons and a red keffiyeh without an iqal approached Ahmad. Ahmad remembered his father's coat. He came closer as if he wanted to whisper something to him. Ahmad walked away, but the man pulled himself closer in his direction. Ahmad said carelessly, "Hello."

The man did not return his greeting. He did not say anything at first, his eyes glancing at a big square between two roads. The city's suffering under the weight of all the displaced people who lived in it was featured in his eyes. He then turned to Ahmad and said, "They will gather here today. If you want, you can run away. They will be harsher today."

Ahmad did not understand what the old man said, his eyes were still not able to decipher the city and its people. He asked the man, "Who are you?"

The man turned his face away from Ahmad in disappointment and muttered, "Who am I?"

He then sighed, turned his face to the gloomy sky, and said in a wounded voice like the screeching of the chains of an old tank on its way to war, "The son of this land, my son. The son of her sin with these traitors, the agents of the sultan. The product of those who decorate the truth for his majesty, and divide the spoils among themselves, in his absence and in his presence. Meanwhile, I wait for a coat that a military camp might discard because its buttons were not shiny enough."

The sun rose and set at the middle of the sky, quickly disappearing, and reappearing, kissed by the passing clouds, like a dancer, placing a veil on her face and removing it every time she shakes her belly.

The old man stopped, then started walking again. Ahmad followed him. He turned around and, while looking into Ahmad's eyes said, "Don't let the desire of revenge make a hero out of you. Leave this place."

Ahmad felt the eyes of the old man penetrating his heart and reading it.

Minutes after Ahmad's encounter with the old mysterious man, his strange look, his chilling words, and surprising warning, the earth shook. Sounds approached like a distant thunder and came closer, little by little. While Ahmad looked for the source of the voices and chants that called for the downfall of everything, heads started to appear from behind the houses that hid the curve of the street leading to the western part of the city.

Crowds approached the place where he was standing with the old man. In minutes, the area was drowned in a wave of colorful human beings, shouting all kinds of slogans against everything.

Ahmad approached a man speaking in the dense crowd while chants filled the air, and thought to himself, "He looks very much like the history teacher, Yusuf. His speech uses the same words, *system*, *constitution*, *government*, *corruption*, and *reform*."

Ahmad tried to raise his head to see above the crowd. A group rushed to a small pickup truck and unloaded a bunch of old tires. One of the organizers yelled something at Ahmad who was consumed with fear. This pulled him out of his silence. Ahmad found himself unconsciously participating in burning the tires.

Suddenly, he paused and noticed, "Nothing has changed. The faces were the same, the names were the same, and the means were the same."

But that day he discovered something different about the people of Ja'far—the people of the south. He saw their swords and daggers that reminded him of the night when he was sold a story by that fat, cunning sheikh. Suddenly he saw the same sheikh moving between the crowd. Ahmad wanted to follow him, but the sheikh disappeared.

The event shook him. He recalled his first meeting with the fat sheikh in his village, more than a year ago. His mind compared that day's promised jihad and today's jihad. What a difference!

At that moment, the Darak attacked the rioters. Ahmad never thought that he ran from one battle to join another. He left Syria because he wanted to regain his health and figure things out.

He noticed a small innocent face wearing a military helmet twice the size of his head. The sight of the young soldier planted doubt and suspicion in Ahmad's head. Ahmad turned his face away ready to run, but something made him look back at the young man again. The Darak surrounded Ahmad, and his eyes met the eyes of the soldier with the innocent face.

"It's Khalid!" Ahmad whispered with a heart shivering with fear and surprise.

It was his brother, Khalid, whom he said goodbye to over a year ago.

Khalid's eyes filled with tears while Ahmad's eyes were begging him for help.

Khalid raised his hand to say goodbye to his brother while his friends' sticks were beating his body. Ahmad fixed his gaze on his brother's image, which was fading under the impact of the beating.

A Darak who hid his face with a black scarf felt victorious when he brought down Ahmad like a fierce lion attacking a wounded gazelle.

A soldier grabbed Ahmad and pushed him into an armored vehicle. Ahmad dragged himself to the small window at the back of the vehicle trying to find his brother. Khalid walked to the window with tears in his yes, while not bringing attention to himself, and said, "Our mother has been looking for you for over a year. Where have you been?"

Then added, "Your mother is dying in grief over you, and you are looking for wealth and fame?

"We are meeting as enemies while the grief is killing our mother, and Abu Khalil is enjoying watching her suffer. Who did that to us?"

Ahmad controlled his fear, looked at his brother and said, "Injustice. I came here by accident. Destiny brought me here. What brought you to this place?"

The young man looked through the large helmet and whispered, "Don't you know that the men from the north serve in the south, and the men from the south serve in the north?"

"Why?" asked Ahmad while wiping the blood from his face.

Khalid looked at his brother, and his heart ached when he saw the condition of his brother but knew that there was nothing he could do at that moment, and relied, "Because they think that, if we from the south serve in the north, we will have no mercy on the people we deal with. People like our drill sergeant think of us as fuel for their battles. Hunger is still what controls everything. Where did you spend the time?"

"In Deraa, near the Syrian border. I do not want to even think about it.

Ahmad wanted to know all about his little brother's life. He asked with a choking voice, and a face covered in blood and tears, "And you, how did you get to be in this regiment, and who put you here?"

Ahmad moved away from the opening. His thoughts and memories were lost in his chains. He thought of the dim light that reflected off the glass pitcher which his uncle, Abu Khalil, stole from the big box like the one he was in now, and he continued to drown in memories, drenched in pain.

Khalid said absentmindedly, "I don't remember, but I do not eat c bread and tea."

Ahmad remembered his brother asking their mother for more tl bread and tea, and a faint smile touched his heart.

The vehicle that held Ahmad and the other protestors drove off wl Khalid was taking off his helmet to say a proper goodbye to his broth He thought, "Is this the enemy of my sergeant, Abu Shafra, and his m(Is my brother, Ahmad, my enemy?"

Meanwhile, Ahmad's eyes were watching the raging crowd throu the small window of the moving vehicle. How the smoke, water canno and the clubs managed to disperse them in a few minutes. Now they w(disappearing through the narrow alleys, to reappear, then disappe again.

A soldier opened a small cell in the big prison, shoved Ahmad's tl body inside, and shut the door behind him.

In the dark cell, Ahmad looked for an opening for air to breath h found none. He searched the cell's cold walls and moist ground and st could not find any.

In the overwhelming silence and absolute darkness, Ahmad's we; body collapsed, and a white cloud covered his sight. He heard the voi(of a soldier saying to him, "Calm down. Calm down. You will not be he long. We will be moving you somewhere else shortly."

The next day, Ahmad heard the rattling of chains and locks and tl squeaking of doors opening and closing but did not see anything. H eyes were losing their sight. Darkness was all around him, and everythin seemed lifeless. His face became pale, his heart became calloused froi the frequent beatings, and his head felt like a heavy rock weighing h body down.

Ahmad was lost in a corner of the prison where darkness prevailec Then, through the darkness, a small opening sent a dim ray of light int(his cell. A faint waft of air came through the opening and, with it, broke words spread throughout the room. "He's still alive."